Cranberry Sage Myrtle Bay Cozy Mystery

By Leena Clover

Copyright © Leena Clover, Author 2020

All rights reserved. No part of this publication may be reproduced, stored in a retrieval system, or transmitted, in any form, or by any means (electronic, mechanical, photocopying, recording or otherwise) without the prior written permission of the author.

This book is a work of fiction. Names, characters, places, organizations and incidents are either products of the author's imagination or used fictitiously. Any resemblance to actual events, places, organizations or persons, living or dead, is entirely coincidental.

First Published – February 23, 2020

Chapter 1

Anna Butler pulled out a tray of steaming cupcakes from the oven. The earthy scent of sage filled the kitchen. Anna closed her eyes and breathed in the heady mix of flavors wafting off the cakes. She set them on a rack to cool and stirred the special cream cheese frosting that would be piped in a swirl on top of the cupcakes.

Anna's granddaughter Meg had christened the cake Cranberry Sage Miracle. Anna agreed it was the perfect name for her holiday creation. The upcoming Christmas season was nothing short of a miracle for Anna. She had a new lease on life after going through a rough period.

Two years ago, Anna had found herself widowed at fifty five. Her husband John had been the love of her life. Before she could come to terms with her grief, she was diagnosed with breast cancer. She fought the disease bravely, supported by her friends and her daughter Cassie. She had barely recovered from the lengthy treatments when she took the plunge and opened her own café, a dream she had cherished all her life.

The people of Dolphin Bay fell in love with Anna's delicious cupcakes. Anna's Café soon became popular with locals and tourists. When her granddaughter Meg unexpectedly came into her life, Anna's cup runneth over.

Anna's daughter had given Meg up for adoption right after she was born. There was no trace of her after that and Anna knew the chances of ever setting eyes on her were slim. Meg's arrival had been momentous and the three Butler women were still coming to terms with it.

Anna was sure of one thing. She had lost count of her blessings. Living under the same roof with her daughter and her granddaughter was a true Christmas miracle.

A tall, attractive woman with curves in all the right places walked into the kitchen. Her shiny mahogany hair was piled on top of her head in an intricate style. She wore a red gown that shimmered as she walked. Diamonds glittered at her ears. All this bling paled before the glow on her face. Cassandra Butler had once been Hollywood's darling, and many a prestigious magazine had crowned her with a 'most beautiful woman' title over the years.

"Why are you still slaving in the kitchen, Mom?" Cassie demanded. "You need to get ready."

Anna bit her lip in concentration as she piped frosting over the cool cupcakes.

"I'm not sure I should go."

"Why not!" Cassie put her hands on her hips and glared at her mother like the diva she was. "You've been working your butt off for the past few weeks. A holiday party is just what you need to unwind a bit."

"Not just any party." Anna looked up at her daughter. "Your grandfather worked for the Gardiners all his life. I wonder if they remember him."

"He was an employee and he got paid for his services," Cassie grunted. "He wasn't their slave, Mom. You are watching too much Downton Abbey."

"We never mingled with them, Cassie." Anna sighed. "I don't want to come across like an upstart."

"Trust me, you won't."

Anna realized her daughter was going to keep at it until she gave in.

The doorbell chimed, distracting both of them.

"I'll get it." Cassie hurried out with a knowing smile on her face.

She was back two minutes later, followed by a tall, hefty man with dark hair and eyes the color of milk chocolate. Anna's face lit up when he smiled at her.

Gino Mancini was many things. Lately, he was Anna's special friend. Gino had retired as the police chief of Dolphin Bay. He now managed the family business, a well known winery his grandfather had started. Mystic Hill was making a name beyond California, thanks to Gino's hard work.

"Do you need some help, Anna? Cassie and I can help clear up while you get ready."

"She's not coming!" Cassie burst out.

"Aren't you well?" Gino's eyes clouded with concern.

"When was your last doctor's appointment?"

"I'm fine." Anna pursed her lips. "I don't really know the Gardiners. Like I was telling Cassie, they have always seemed a bit hoity-toity to me. I don't exactly have an invite, do I?"

"They are nothing of the sort." Gino laughed off Anna's concern. "The Gardiners are very friendly. You'll see for yourself when you meet them. And what do you mean you are not invited? You are going as my date."

"That's right, Mom. And Meg's going to be mine."

Anna pulled her apron off reluctantly. Her eyes brightened as a svelte young woman came into the kitchen.

"You're not ready?" she raised her eyebrows. "I thought I was holding you up."

Meg had filled out a bit since she moved in with Anna and Cassie. She had lost the gaunt, waif like look she had sported when she first came to Dolphin Bay, thanks to Anna's home cooked meals. Anna was pleased to note she looked more confident too. Her slouch had disappeared, so had the circles under her eyes. She looked deceptively young, her petite frame making her look sixteen rather than twenty.

"We have plenty of time, kiddo." Gino bent down a bit as Meg stood on her toes to greet him with a kiss.

Anna felt three pairs of eyes give her a questioning look.

"Okay, Okay. Why don't you taste this latest batch of

cupcakes while I put on a dress? Nothing fancy though."

"You won't wear your Christmas sweater, will you?" Cassie was aghast. "Save it for the ugly sweater contest."

"Why don't you wait and see?" Anna asked impishly as she sailed into her bedroom.

The kitchen door flew open as a heavy, imposing woman came in, slightly out of breath. Her blue eyes narrowed as they took in the group in the kitchen.

"We're late. Where's Anna?"

"She just went in to get ready, Aunt Julie." Cassie hugged the portly woman and blew her a kiss.

Anna came out just then, dressed in a simple black silk frock and her favorite string of pearls.

"I hope this is good enough for the Gardiners."

She smoothed her hands over her dress and looked inquiringly at Cassie.

"You look nice, Mom." Cassie smiled reassuringly at her mother.

"Amazing!" Meg breathed. "Don't you agree, Gino?"

Anna felt Gino's eyes on her and sensed a blush steal over her cheeks.

"Since when did you start obsessing over your looks,

Anna?" Julie demanded. "Is Cassie rubbing off on you?"

Julie Walsh was one of Anna's best friends, an integral part of the trio that had christened themselves the Firecrackers. She had known Anna since before Cassie was born and could read her like a book.

"Mom's in awe of the Gardiners," Cassie supplied.

"They might be one of the richest families on the coast," Julie nodded. "But they are very friendly, Anna. Edward Gardiner is a jolly old fellow."

"That's exactly what I was telling her," Gino added. "Shall we go now?"

"How do you know them, Julie?" Meg asked.

"Don't forget Julie's a famous romance author," Anna reminded her. "These rich people like to surround themselves with celebrities. That's probably why they invited Cassie."

"I'm hardly a celebrity now," Cassie sighed. "I've been living here in obscurity for the past year, Mom. Hollywood has forgotten me."

"You will always be Cassandra Butler, Oscar award winner." Anna patted her daughter on the back. "You're the local kid who went away and made it big."

"Made. Past tense, Mom." Cassie sounded bitter. "I'm a nobody now. A has-been."

Anna felt a pang of guilt. Cassie had fallen on hard times

when her business manager took most of her money and ran. When Anna fell ill, Cassie had set her failing career aside and come back to Dolphin Bay to nurse her. She had been at a loose end ever since, looking for the right role that would help her make a grand comeback.

"Stop it, you two!" Julie thundered. "We've all had a long year. But the holidays are here and it's time to let go and relax."

"We do have a lot to celebrate this year," Anna placed an arm around Cassie and Meg as they walked out.

Gino was going to drive them to the party in his luxury sedan. He opened the passenger door for Anna while the others settled into the back seat. Christmas music filled the car as Gino eased out of Anna's driveway. A full moon hung over the Pacific Ocean as they drove along the coast, singing along with the music.

"Will they have a Christmas tree?" Meg asked curiously.

"Just wait and see," Julie smiled. "You're in for a treat."

"When are we getting our tree, Mom?" Cassie asked.

Anna's face fell.

"I never got a tree after your father died. I think it's time to change that."

Chapter 2

Anna looked around eagerly as Gino drove through a pair of massive iron gates. A winding road cut through trees twinkling with hundreds of fairy lights. Gino pulled up under a grand portico and handed over the car to a valet. He helped Anna out of the car and tucked her arm in his.

"Wow!" Meg exclaimed loudly, echoing Anna's thoughts. "This place is even more impressive than yours, Gino."

"Not bad." Cassie looked around. "I didn't know such a place existed in Dolphin Bay."

A short, stocky man dressed in a black suit stepped outside and bowed. His pot belly indicated a taste for rich food. Anna immediately warmed to him. She appreciated people who gave justice to good cooking.

"Hello!" Gino nodded at the red bow tie the man wore. "Getting in the holiday spirit, huh?"

The man gave a slight nod and ushered them inside.

"I expected Edward Gardiner to be taller," Anna whispered.

Gino laughed.

"That's George Pearson, the butler. Believe me, when you see Edward, you'll have no doubt he's king of this castle."

A server stood at the entrance, holding a tray of champagne flutes. There was a sparkling red drink for the abstainers. They each grabbed a drink and walked in, marveling at the twelve foot tall tree that stood in the foyer.

Anna's eyes were wide and her mouth hung open in wonder. She tried to guess how many days it had taken to decorate that massive fir. Dozens of ornaments adorned the tree, sparkling and twinkling under the enormous chandelier that hung in the foyer.

Cassie stepped forward and touched some of the ornaments.

"I think these are real gold!"

"Quite possible," Gino told them. "The Gardiners are loaded."

George Pearson cleared his throat.

"You are right, Madam. Some of these ornaments are almost a hundred years old, bought by the first Mr. Gardiner. They are locked in a special vault and only brought out during the holidays."

The butler cleared his throat again and started climbing a winding staircase leading up to the second floor.

"The Christmas party is always held in the ballroom," he explained. "Some of the guests have already arrived."

A tall, broad shouldered man with a mop of thick brown hair rushed forward to greet them. He hugged Gino and patted him heartily on the back. Emerald eyes full of laughter gave him a once over.

"How are you, my boy?" the man thundered. "We need to finish that last game."

He beamed at all of them.

"Played chess with his father. Gino always tagged along with him when he was a kid. Now he honors me with a game every other Tuesday."

Anna gave Gino a surprised look. She didn't know he liked chess.

"And you must be the gal he can't stop talking about," Edward continued, making Anna blush. "It's hard to find love once in this lifetime. I was blessed with my Beth. But if you're lucky enough to fall in love twice, hold on tight, dearie. Don't let this one go."

"We won't let her," Cassie drawled. "Right, Meg?"

Edward shifted his attention to Cassie.

"Cassandra Butler! You are more stunning in person. Your grandpa called you a diva."

"You remember my father?" Anna couldn't hide her surprise.

"Of course I do. Man worked for us his whole life. Saved us millions in taxes. I can see he passed some of those smarts on to you."

"You're too kind." Anna couldn't hide her grin.

"I'm a regular customer of Anna's Café," Edward declared. "We get a box of your cupcakes every other day. Have them with my tea. I hope you're coming up with a special for Christmas."

Anna started telling him about the cranberry sage recipe she was working on. Cassie nudged her gently and pulled Meg forward.

"May I introduce my daughter Meg, Mr. Gardiner?"

Edward pulled Meg into a hug and patted her cheek.

"Another beauty!" he guffawed, making Meg laugh. "You must meet my granddaughter. She's about your age."

"Are you talking about me, Gramps?"

A willowy young woman dressed in a red mermaid gown joined them. She was as tall as Edward, towering over Cassie and Julie. Her emerald eyes were the same as the old man's. Anna decided the single dimple they both sported was a family trait.

"Dior?" She looked admiringly at Cassie's dress. "I'm wearing Chanel tonight."

"This is Alison, my dearest granddaughter." Edward's voice was laced with pride as he introduced the young girl. "She's taking care of the Gardiner business almost single handedly now. Doing a fantastic job of it too. Profits are up 10% this quarter."

"It's time for you to retire, Gramps," Alison said lovingly. "I hope that's the big announcement you're going to make this Christmas."

"I've still got some steam left in me, girl. Don't put me to sleep yet."

"She might have a point, Edward," Gino remarked. "How old will you be this year? Eighty?"

"Eighty going on eighteen," Edward winked. "I will retire when they carry me out in a body bag."

"Hush, Edward! How many times have I told you to mind what you say?"

Anna blinked as another tall woman with emerald eyes the same shade as Edward's and Alison's joined them. Her left dimple and brown hair immediately suggested she was related to the Gardiners. Anna noted how all of them were over six feet tall. Sharon's curves were more generous than Alison's and the few crow's feet around her eyes pointed at her age. But she looked every bit as attractive as Alison.

"This is my sister Sharon." Edward introduced them. "My wayward younger sister," he added with a laugh and turned toward Sharon. "You already know Gino. These are the Butlers. Anna, Cassie and Meg. And Julie Walsh, of course."

Sharon flashed a hundred watt smile and welcomed them.

"I'm a big fan, Cassie!" she cooed. "When is your next movie coming out?"

"Soon," Cassie muttered, pasting a smile on her face.

Sharon chatted with Julie next, telling her what she liked about her latest book. A few servers descended on them with trays loaded with a wide variety of canapés, ranging from everyone's favorite crab puffs to dates stuffed with goat cheese and wrapped in bacon.

Anna finally had a chance to check out the other guests. She spotted a few familiar faces. The ballroom was humungous in dimension, surrounded by a wraparound balcony overlooking some craggy cliffs and the ocean beyond. The dome shaped ceiling towered twenty feet high, hung with crystal chandeliers. Garlands of holly were woven artistically. Mistletoe was placed over strategic spots and couples giggled and kissed sportingly when caught standing under it.

Anna shivered suddenly when her eyes landed on a smartly dressed woman deep in conversation with a tall, blonde man. The woman turned around just then, her malevolent gaze flashing fire at Anna.

"Just ignore her," Gino said softly and led Anna to the buffet table.

"Planning to kill someone again?" A voice hissed in her ear, making Anna drop the plate she had just picked up. "Who invited you, Anna? This is no place for riff raff."

Anna ignored the vile woman. Lara Crawford was the mayor of Dolphin Bay. She was convinced Anna had murdered her husband John. Her position of power meant the locals listened to her. Anna had suffered a lot because of her allegations until Gino came into her life. They were working on finding out the truth about what had happened to John. But solving a two year old murder wasn't easy. Meanwhile, they had no choice but to ignore Lara as she went about hazing Anna.

The band started playing some catchy tunes and Edward encouraged everyone to dance. Gino pulled Anna onto the floor and twirled her around. She focused her full attention on him after making sure Cassie, Meg and Julie had all found dancing partners.

Champagne flowed and a lavish roast dinner was served, along with chestnut stuffing and an array of roasted, steamed and fried vegetables. The butler carved the meat and Edward stood next to him, playing the consummate host, urging everyone to take second helpings. A pudding was brought out, doused in rum and flambéed while the guests applauded.

Toast after toast followed. Edward Gardiner told a few jokes, making everyone laugh. He hinted heavily at the big surprise he had in store for everyone on Christmas day. Anna wondered what the old man had up his sleeve.

"Do you know what he's talking about?" she asked Gino.

"Not this time." Gino was thoughtful. "Edward often consults me before making any business decisions. Maybe he is really planning to retire."

"He's so full of life," Anna sighed. "I hope I'm like him when I reach his age. That is, if I live that long."

Gino snuggled closer to her, placing an arm around her shoulders.

"You're not getting away just yet, Anna Butler. I have big plans for us."

They both whirled around as giggles erupted behind them. Cassie and Meg stood arm in arm, blushing and laughing their heads off.

Anna didn't think she could be happier. Her family was together again and everyone seemed to be getting along. Her friendship with Gino was progressing well, making her believe she might have a second chance at love. This Christmas season was full of miracles.

Chapter 3

Anna sat in her garden three days later, sipping a cup of coffee. She had been up since five, baking cakes and sweets for her café. A busy day loomed ahead and Anna cherished the brief respite she enjoyed before breakfast.

The café was doing brisk business in the holiday season. Dolphin Bay rarely had a white Christmas but there was no shortage of yuletide spirit in the seaside town. The December temperatures had dropped to the 50s, allowing people to show off their winter clothing. Anna ran out of cupcakes by noon most days and had to turn people away.

She shivered in her coat and rushed back inside, ready to begin her day.

Cassie sat at the kitchen table, eating frosted flakes. Meg was stirring eggs on the stove. A plate of avocado toast sat on the table, ready to be eaten. Anna sprinkled some hot sauce on the toast and bit into it.

"You're spoiling me." She smiled as Meg placed the cheesy scrambled eggs before her. "I could get used to this. What will I do when you go off to college?"

Cassie cleared her throat.

"Are you saying I can't scramble eggs, Mom?" She had a twinkle in her eye.

"It's not like you will stay here forever either, Cassie. You'll be flying to Hollywood the moment someone offers you the right role."

Anna and Meg rushed through breakfast and started loading the van. Ten minutes later, they pulled up before a massive storefront overlooking the bay. Anna had owned and operated Bayside Books for twenty years. She had opened her café in the adjoining space, occupying a prime spot at the corner of Main Street. Both her shops offered a priceless view of the Coastal Walk and the water and were becoming very popular as news of her baking prowess spread.

Anna started brewing coffee while Meg began setting up the display cases.

The café door flew open and a harried balding man with grey hair growing out of his ears rushed in. He had taught English at the high school all his life. Now he was the editor of the Dolphin Bay Chronicle.

"Good Morning, Ian," Anna greeted him. "I'll have your latte and cupcake ready in a minute."

"The coffee can wait." Ian rubbed his bald head and stared at Anna. "I have some bad news, Anna."

Anna felt a weight on her chest.

"Is Cassie alright? She was fine twenty minutes ago."

"What?" Ian's eyes grew wider. "I don't know anything about Cassie. This is about Edward Gardiner."

"What about him?" Anna asked, thinking of the jovial old man she had met recently.

"Edward Gardiner is dead. I just heard it on the police scanner."

"That sweet old man!" Anna cried. "He looked perfectly healthy three days ago."

"I don't think he got sick, Anna," Ian said meaningfully. "Someone called the police for a reason."

"You suspect foul play?" Anna was aghast.

"It's too early to say anything. We will have to wait and watch. I'll take that coffee now, if you don't mind. I need to start working on this right away. It's front page material."

A stream of customers came in and Anna barely noticed Ian leave. She almost forgot about Edward until her friends Julie and Mary arrived. The Firecrackers had met at Anna's bookstore at least once a day for several years. They had continued the tradition even after Anna opened the café.

Julie looked sober and was quiet for a change. Mary was sad.

"Ian Samuels told me." Anna sat next to Mary at their usual window table.

"He did a lot of good for the community, you know." Julie's voice was heavy. "Edward always made me laugh. He was so full of life, Anna. Why would someone hurt him?"

"Are you sure that's what happened, Julie?"

"That's the rumor going around," Mary explained. "Maybe we should go to the Yellow Tulip for lunch?" She referred to the local diner which was the hotbed of gossip in town.

"Have you talked to Gino?" Julie asked. "He was close to the Gardiners."

Anna looked stricken. "I didn't think of that. He must be devastated."

Anna placed a call to Gino. As she had expected, he was at the Gardiner mansion, paying his respects to the family. He promised to catch up with her later.

"Poor Alison," Mary clucked. "Sharon is the only family she has left now."

"You know Alison Gardiner?" Anna was surprised.

"Not very well," Mary admitted. "Her sister Ruth went to school with my daughter. Alison used to tag along with her sometimes."

"Ruth doesn't live in Dolphin Bay?"

"Ruth died in childbirth two years ago," Mary explained, making Anna gasp.

"Look at the turn this day's taken," Julie sighed. "We've forgotten all about Sofia."

Anna snorted.

"Believe me! That's not possible."

"When does she get here?" Mary asked.

"Are you talking about Nana?" Meg asked eagerly, placing a plate of the cranberry sage cupcakes before them. "I'm so looking forward to meeting her."

Anna's mother Sofia was pushing 80. She had relocated to a senior community in sunny Southern California ten years ago when Anna's father passed. She was thriving in the warm climate, raising hell with her cronies a few miles from the Mexico border.

Sofia descended on Dolphin Bay for Christmas every year, armed with plenty of helpful advice for Anna. She had skipped her visit for the past two years due to some unavoidable snafus. Anna had never told her mother about her illness. But it paled in comparison to the big secret she had kept from her for the past twenty years.

"Does she know yet?" Julie whispered, tipping her head at Meg's back.

"She doesn't," Anna sighed loudly. "Neither does Mom."

"You're in hot water, Anna," Julie warned. "You better be ready for the sky to fall in."

Mary stroked Anna's back.

"Don't you listen to her. I'm sure Sofia will understand."

"Have you met my mother?" Anna rolled her eyes. "In this case, I can't blame her. I shouldn't have listened to Cassie."

"You were protecting her," Mary soothed.

"Are you talking about me?" Cassie asked, walking in through the bookstore.

To Anna's astonishment, Cassie had given up hanging out by the pool and started helping out at the bookstore, easing some of her load.

"We're talking about your Nana," Julie told her. "Have you thought about how you're going to handle her?"

"I haven't met her for five years. Surely she's mellowed a bit with age?"

"When are you going to tell Meg?" Anna asked. "You need to prepare her for the worst."

"You really think Nana won't accept Meg?" Cassie asked worriedly. "We have solid proof that Meg is really my kid."

Julie's eyebrows shot up.

"Look who's talking, girls. How long did it take you to warm up to her, Cassie?"

Meg had come back to clear the plates. Anna realized she had heard their entire conversation. Meg's eyes were huge as she sidled closer to her mother.

"Cassie and I are just getting to know each other. It will be the same with Nana. Don't worry. I don't have any fantastic expectations."

Anna's eyes glistened with tears. She pulled Meg and Cassie in for a hug.

"I spent twenty years longing for this moment, girls. Promise me you'll stay in touch no matter where your life leads you."

"Oh Anna!" Meg cried. "I've just found you! I'm not letting you go."

"She's right, Mom." Cassie squeezed Anna's shoulder. "Dolphin Bay is my home. I'll always come back here."

"Thanks girls." Anna wiped a tear furtively. "Let's hope my mother goes easy on us."

Meg smiled.

"I used to dream about having a grandma. Now I get a Nana as a bonus! I'm going to love her no matter how she feels about me."

"This is what I hate about Christmas!" Julie butted in, making the others gasp. "Everyone gets emotional all the time and starts crying."

Anna punched her arm in jest.

Neither of them noticed Gino come in.

"Can a man get some coffee here?" he asked wearily.

"I'll get it." Meg rushed to get him a fresh cup.

"I talked to Leo," Gino volunteered, referring to his nephew who had recently joined the Dolphin Bay police force. "The police are tight lipped now but they are definitely treating Edward's death as suspicious."

Anna's hand flew to her mouth.

"That poor man! I hope he didn't suffer."

"He died in his sleep. Cause of death is suffocation, or asphyxiation, to be precise."

"His family must be devastated," Anna murmured.

"I think they are still in shock." Gino shook his head. "I was going to play chess with him today."

"How can we help?" Julie asked. "The Gardiners were so nice to everyone, I can't imagine something like this happening to them."

"I think I met him for a reason," Anna spoke up.

"We let the police do their job." Gino gave Anna a meaningful look. "You have enough on your plate with the holiday rush and your mother's visit. I suggest you sit this one out, Anna."

Chapter 4

Anna tried to concentrate as she swirled cream cheese frosting on her cupcakes. She felt like snuggling under the covers and taking the whole month off. Why did the holidays always have to be so stressful?

The Butler household had experienced drama worthy of a prime time soap opera the previous day. Sofia arrived on a cloud of perfume, wearing a red pant suit Anna remembered from the 90s. She had examined Anna and Cassie from head to toe and muttered about how thin they both looked. Then she commandeered the kitchen and proceeded to stir the pots that had been cooking on the stove.

Lunch had been a boisterous affair with Julie and Mary in attendance. Meg was introduced as a guest. Sofia's eyes had narrowed as she gave the young girl a onceover. She barely spoke to her through the extravagant meal. Anna took matters in hand over dessert.

"What do you mean, she's your granddaughter?" Sofia's voice was hoarse. "Did one of your foster kids have a child?"

Anna shook her head.

"Meg's our flesh and blood."

Cassie grabbed Anna's wrist and gave her a supportive

look.

"Meg is my daughter, Nana. I gave birth to her when I was sixteen."

Sofia was turning red.

"I may be getting older, girls, but my memory is intact. How do I not remember this?"

"We never told you," Cassie admitted. "It's my fault, Nana. If you have to blame anyone, blame me."

"Where has this child been all these years?" Sofia was staring at Meg, her face full of anguish.

Anna poured out the whole story about Meg's adoption and her subsequent years in foster care. Meg stared at the floor without saying a word.

Sofia struggled to her feet and walked out of the room. Julie sprang up and followed her. She called Anna an hour later to let her know Sofia was safe and was camped at her house for the immediate future.

Meg had been stoic, Cassie furious. Anna had lamely assured them Sofia would come around.

Meg walked into the kitchen, her hair still wet from the shower.

"I made pancakes," Anna told her. "Lemon, ricotta and blueberry. Just get the maple syrup from the pantry."

"Thanks Anna!" Meg gave her a hug. "You're spoiling me rotten."

She dug into her pancakes and smacked her lips in approval.

"Nana's justified, you know. Don't be too hard on her."

The phone rang, cutting off Anna's response. Her face brightened when she heard Gino's deep, comforting voice and she tucked a strand of hair behind her ear.

"Nothing has changed since yesterday," she reported. "Mom's maintaining radio silence and is still at Julie's."

Her jaw dropped after hearing what Gino had to say.

"That's confirmed then. It's a murder investigation."

She hung up and sat down at the table.

"Did Gino have an update on Mr. Gardiner?" Meg asked.

"The police found some peculiar residue in his nostrils. They are thinking someone put a plastic bag over his head, Meg."

"That's awful!" Meg cried. "Who would want to harm him? Don't you want to know, Anna?"

"The police are looking into it. Teddy Fowler must be on the case."

"We know how useful he has been in the past." Meg stared at Anna. "We need someone with your sleuthing skills."

"It's the holidays." Anna shrugged. "I barely knew the man, sweetie. I have enough on my hands with the café and your Nana."

"I guess," Meg shrugged.

"When are you going to the university? They'll be closing for the holidays any time now."

"I'm going there today," Meg confirmed. "Can you manage without me for a couple of hours?"

"Don't worry about me," Anna assured her. "Your college applications are more important. You are cutting it fine, as it is."

Meg clammed up. Anna was pleased to see she looked a bit miffed. That meant she was slowly coming out of her shell and behaving like a normal teenager.

Later that morning, Anna couldn't stop thinking of the Gardiners. She had barely had time to take a break. She glanced at the grandmother clock near the entrance, surprised to see it was almost 11 AM. Mary was visiting her daughter in San Jose. Anna wondered if Julie would make an appearance, with or without Sofia.

She looked up eagerly as the bell behind the door jingled. She tried to hide her disappointment when she realized it wasn't her mother.

"Expecting someone else?" A short, wiry man with a shock of thick white hair asked.

Anna recognized the man as the owner of the wine shop behind Paradise Market. He had never come to the café before. She tried not to stare at the vivid red cardigan he wore, embroidered with reindeer and snowflakes.

"Come in, come in." She gave him a welcoming smile. "How can I help you?"

"Anna Butler, I presume?" he asked, coming up to the counter. "It is I who is going to help you."

"Pardon me?" Anna frowned.

"I'm Craig Rose. Can we sit and talk?"

The cafe was experiencing a rare lull. Anna decided the young couple deep in conversation at a corner table wouldn't need her for a while. She took off her apron, poured two cups of coffee and ushered the odd man to a window table.

"What do you know about Edward Gardiner?" he asked point blank.

Anna tried to hide her surprise.

"He owns Gardiner Fishing Supply. I guess he was one of the richest men in town. My …"

The man held up a hand, cutting her off.

"Let's not beat around the bush. Word on the street is that you are some kind of amateur sleuth. You helped the police solve some local murders."

Anna sipped her coffee, guessing the man wasn't done.

"I want you to find out who killed Edward Gardiner."

"I'm sorry to disappoint you, Mr. Rose, but I have my hands full here. This is a new venture and the holidays are a busy time for us."

"I'll pay you well."

"I don't charge money! I was just helping my friends."

"Don't you want to know what I'm offering?" Craig Rose leaned forward dramatically.

"What?" Anna spluttered.

"Information. Worth more than its weight in gold."

"I don't understand."

"Rumor around town is you killed your husband."

Anna folded her hands and glared at the man before her.

"I think you should leave now."

Craig Rose ignored her. He picked up his coffee cup with both hands and took a deep sip.

"I know something about John."

"I don't believe you knew him. My John never mentioned you."

"You think your husband told you everything?" Craig smirked.

Anna tried to forget the shameful secret she had recently uncovered about her husband. Maybe he hadn't always been upfront with her.

"Go snooping around like you usually do. Find out who killed Edward."

"What do you know about John?" Anna demanded. "If you know something pertaining to his death, you should tell the police."

"Are you sure about that?" Craig smiled maliciously.

"I don't care for innuendo." Anna was cross. "Just spit it out, mister."

Craig rolled up the sleeves of his cardigan.

"I do have your best interests at heart, Mrs. Butler. Anna. Believe me. I just need your help."

"Why do you care about the Gardiners?" Anna asked.

"Have you met Finn O'Malley?"

"Never heard of him," Anna responded impatiently.

"Finn married Edward's granddaughter Ruth. The police are eyeing him as a suspect. I find that ridiculous, of course."

"You care about this Finn?" Anna thought back to the

party at the Gardiners'. She wondered if Finn was the blue eyed man who had been talking to Lara Crawford.

"Finn and my son were posted in the same unit in Afghanistan. They saw a lot of action. The inevitable happened. My son died in combat. Finn was injured trying to save him. He brought my son home."

"I'm sorry to hear that."

Anna felt a connection with Craig Rose. They had both lost someone they loved dearly.

"Finn is the only family I have now." Craig's voice wavered. "He's an honorable man, a decorated veteran. If he wanted to kill someone, he would shoot them point blank in the chest."

"So you believe he's capable of murder?" Anna cried.

"Don't you twist my words. I'm offering a simple barter. You help clear Finn. I will tell you a shocking truth about your husband."

"I need to think this over," Anna said grudgingly. "Even if I decide to help you, I can't promise anything. I'm not Sherlock Holmes."

"As long as your efforts are sincere ..." Craig stood up. "Don't take too long. And I'd rather you didn't let anyone in on our arrangement. Not even Finn."

Anna couldn't decide if Craig Rose was evil or desperate. Maybe he was jumping ahead. Did the police really think the grandson-in-law was a suspect?

Meg rushed in, looking indignant.

"I'll have to think twice about applying to DBU. You won't believe what happened today, Anna."

Chapter 5

Anna got off the phone. Sally Davis, a teacher at the local high school had called.

"What does Sally want, Mom?" Cassie asked.

The Butler women were gathered around the breakfast table. Cassie was dressed in workout clothes, drinking orange juice before going for a run. Meg appeared moody, playing with the avocado toast on her plate.

"She called to remind us of the tree lighting ceremony tonight. It's in the town square at seven."

Cassie looked uncertain.

"Do you really want to go? Lara Crawford will be there, probably. You know what that means."

"Your father and I never missed the tree lighting ceremony. It's a tradition, Cassie. I'm not changing the way I live my life just because of one nasty person."

"So what?" Cassie scoffed. "Everyone just stands there while someone flips a switch? Sounds silly to me."

"You and your Hollywood ways," Anna clucked. "These things are important to us. Almost everyone turns up for the tree lighting. There's hot cider and cocoa. The Holiday

Committee works really hard to decorate the tree and the town square."

"Whatever you say, Mom."

"You'd rather sit at home and watch something on television?" Anna placed her hands on her hips. "Or gossip with Bobby, I guess."

"Bobby's not back from his trip to Costa Rica," Cassie grumbled, referring to her friend who was a fitness trainer to the stars in Los Angeles. "I haven't really talked to him in a while."

"I can stay home with you," Meg offered. "I hardly know anyone in town."

"Which is why you should go," Anna said sternly. "And you have met a lot of the locals at the café by now. I want to show you off, Meg."

"I'm reading a script, actually," Cassie volunteered. "It's a good role. But don't get your hopes up."

"Why didn't you say so before?" Anna asked. "Does it have to be read tonight?"

"Not really," Cassie sighed. "I give up, Mom. I'll go with you to the tree lighting, okay? Now, can I please go on my run? Pretty please?"

Anna and Meg laughed and Cassie joined in.

"Do you think you'll run into Teddy Fowler?" Anna asked seriously.

"I usually do," Cassie shrugged. "Why?"

"No reason. Just wondered how he's doing with the Gardiner case."

"You want me to chat him up and pump him for information."

"Can you?" Anna sounded eager.

"I'll see what I can do." Cassie stretched her arms over her head and took a deep breath. "When are you going to start working out with me, Meg?"

Meg had been dozing at the table.

"Huh … what?" she snapped awake.

"What's the matter with you, child?" Anna asked. "You've been preoccupied since yesterday."

"Did something happen?" Cassie asked, stretching her hamstring. "How did things go at the university?"

"I totally forgot!" Anna exclaimed. "You were looking all riled up when you got back from DBU yesterday. Did someone give you a hard time, sweetie?"

Anna vaguely remembered Meg complaining about something. A flood of tourists had come in just then and they both got busy. She had never had a chance to ask her what she meant.

Meg squirmed as Anna and Cassie both stared at her.

"The weirdest thing happened. I was on my way to the admissions building when a guy grabbed me."

"In broad daylight?" Anna was aghast.

"I hope you fought back," Cassie bristled.

Meg looked contrite. "I was too shocked to do anything."

"That's it. You're taking self defense classes. Bobby can come here and teach you himself."

"Let the girl speak, Cassie," Anna interrupted. "What did he want, Meg?"

"That's the weird thing," Meg replied. "This guy was leading some kind of protest with a bunch of other kids. They were holding handmade signs and posters. Some stuff about saving the environment, I think."

"Go on," Anna prompted.

"He wanted me to hold one end of a big banner. Said one of their protestors hadn't turned up."

"Sounds crazy alright," Cassie murmured.

"I stood there waving that banner for almost half an hour. The guy was right next to me, making sure I wouldn't leave."

"Was he good looking?" Cassie's face curved in a smile. "I wouldn't mind being kidnapped by a hunk."

"Spare us your nonsense, Cassie. Can't you see the poor

child is traumatized?"

"I'm fine, Anna." Meg wrung a hand through her hair. "I'm just angry. I mean, how dare he!"

"Did you get his name?" Anna wanted to know. "We can talk to Leo about this. Ask him to have a few words with this man."

"He's not a man." Meg squinted her eyes as if trying to remember. "Must be my age. I guess he's a student at DBU. I heard someone refer to him as Phoenix."

"What kind of name is that?" Anna muttered.

"Forget about his name." Cassie started jogging on spot. "Tell us what happened after that."

"Nothing! They chanted some slogans for a while and then the group disbanded. Everyone kind of dispersed in different directions, including that guy. He didn't even say Thank You!"

Anna placed a hand on Meg's shoulder.

"Forget about it. Not worth your time."

"You mean it was a waste of time," Meg said hotly. "My arm's been sore all night and the admissions office closed by the time I got there."

"You can go there today," Anna comforted her. "I can manage at the café. Cassie will help me."

"Sure!" Cassie nodded. "It's kinda late to go for a run now anyway. I can take a quick shower and go to the café with you guys."

The kitchen door burst open and Sofia marched in, holding a wet umbrella. Anna had barely noticed it had started raining. Julie came in after Sofia. She gave a slight shrug in response to Anna's questioning glance.

"Hello Nana!" Cassie said cheerfully. "We weren't expecting you."

"Don't be cheeky, young lady," Sofia glared. She trained her gaze on Anna. "Now, are we going to sit somewhere like civilized people or do you want to keep your old mama standing in the kitchen?"

Anna stopped gaping and ushered her mother out to the living room. Julie followed with Cassie and Meg. Sofia sat in a chair by the fireplace and quivered. Anna rushed to light the electric fire and went inside to get a hot drink for her mother. Sofia only drank cocoa.

"I don't suppose you have any biscotti?" Sofia grumbled when Anna offered her a plate of assorted cookies. "I see you have forgotten your Italian roots."

"I'm sorry, Mama," Anna said meekly. "We ran out of it."

"Anna makes the best biscotti," Meg burst out. "I ate it all."

Sofia shook her head in disapproval.

"You can't even pronounce it right. What kind of cultural education are you giving her, Anna?"

Anna folded her hands and sat down on a couch facing her mother.

"Meg just got here, Mom. We had a lot to catch up on."

"What's more important than your culture, Anna?" She pointed at Meg. "This child needs to know where she came from."

"Stop giving Mom a hard time, Nana." Cassie stepped in. "Tell us what you're doing here."

Sofia blew on her cocoa and drained half the cup. Three pairs of eyes stared at her hopefully.

"I did some heavy thinking and I have come to a decision."

Cassie and Meg wove their hands through Anna's and waited with bated breath.

"I don't know what the future holds. At my age, every day is a blessing. What's done is done, although it pains me."

"I'm sorry, Nana. I should never have given Meg away. I know that now. But I was a foolish sixteen year old with stars in my eyes. What did I know?"

"It's all my fault, Mama. Cassie was ignorant, like she says. She was a child herself. But I should have known better. John and I really wanted to keep the baby but we gave in. And we shouldn't have hidden this from you."

Meg said nothing. She had already forgiven Anna and Cassie. There was no point in rehashing what might have been. She just hoped her Nana would see that. She didn't want to cause a rift in the family.

"That's enough!" Sofia held up her hand. "Enough time has been wasted."

She opened her arms and looked at Meg.

"Come here, child."

Meg flew into the old woman's arms. Cassie joined her a split second later.

Julie sat down next to Anna and offered her a tissue. Anna laughed as her nose ran and tears streamed down her eyes.

"This Christmas is full of miracles," she mumbled through her tears.

The doorbell chimed. Julie leapt up and flung the front door open. Gino came in and looked around, bewildered.

"Is something wrong, Anna? I went to the café but it was closed. So I came here."

"The café!" Anna exclaimed. "Meg, we need to go right now."

There was a flurry of activity after that. Sofia grilled Gino while the ladies loaded the van with trays of cookies and cupcakes. Her face broke into a smile when she learned Gino was Italian.

"You are going to help me cook a proper Italian meal," she told him. "Look how skinny my girls are. I need to put some meat on their bones."

Chapter 6

"I never thought my mother would come around so soon." Anna still felt a bit dazed as she sat drinking coffee with the Firecrackers. "Do you remember how furious she was?"

"You didn't expect her to just fall in line, did you?" Julie took Sofia's side. "Imagine the shock she must have felt."

Gino came in before Anna had a chance to reply.

"Hello ladies!"

"Looks like you escaped from Sofia's clutches," Julie laughed. "I bet she gave you the third degree."

"I expect nothing less from a concerned mother. She's just looking out for Anna."

"Did you remind her you were the chief of police?" Anna asked. "You'll keep me safe."

"Always!" Gino sat down with the women.

Mary spoke up. She was the quiet one of the group but was extremely astute.

"You look like you have something on your mind, Gino."

Gino picked up the cup of coffee Anna poured for him and nodded.

"I'm supposed to be on a grocery run for Sofia. But I wanted to discuss something with you ladies."

"It's about Edward Gardiner, isn't it?" Anna guessed.

"Sharon called me last night. The whole family is under scrutiny and she wants me to prove they are innocent."

"Do you believe her?" Anna asked. "About all of them being innocent, I mean."

"I don't really know them well," Gino admitted. "I did visit the old man frequently but I rarely spent any time with the others."

"So you can't make such a blanket promise, Gino."

"That's what I told her, Anna. I'm willing to look into it but I can't promise what I'll find."

The Firecrackers nodded.

"It's always good to be upfront," Mary said. "So what did Sharon say? Did she agree to your condition?"

"Reluctantly." Gino bit into a cupcake. "She says she has nothing to hide."

"We'll see about that." Anna folded her arms and looked up as Cassie came in through the bookstore.

"I thought you were not going to get involved in this murder business, Mom." She turned to Gino. "No offense, Gino, but she's got a lot going on."

"I can do most of the leg work. But it will be nice to consult Anna. Your mother's one smart cookie, Cassie. I could use her analytical skills."

"Hear, hear." Julie bumped a fist in the air. "That's a first. They make a good team, Cassie. You have nothing to worry about."

"All I'm saying is …"

"Enough!" Anna said sharply. "Stop trying to rule my life, Cass. I don't tell you how to live yours."

"But what about your to-do list?" Cassie cried. "We haven't even decorated the stores yet. And we need to get a tree this year. We need to do Christmas right. It's Meg's first Christmas at home, Mom."

"We'll do everything," Anna assured her. "You'll see."

"And what about your quarterly checkup with the oncologist?" Cassie demanded. "You better not forget about it."

"We won't let her, girl," Julie stepped in. "I've got it marked on my calendar."

"Do you think I won't take care of your mother?" Gino asked Cassie. "Nothing means more to me than Anna's well being."

Cassie had no answer for that. She spun on her heels and went back to the bookstore, grabbing the last cookie on the plate on her way out.

"I apologize for my daughter, Gino."

"No need. She's just looking out for you."

"Enough of the family drama," Julie sighed. "Where do we start?"

"Edward died in his house, right?" Anna asked. "I think we should start by making a list of how many people live there."

"I can help you with that," Gino offered, pulling out a pen and a small notepad from his pocket.

Julie whipped out her iPad from her bag and offered it to Gino.

"You can use this."

"I prefer the old fashioned way," Gino grinned. "Now let's see. There's Pearson, the butler, of course."

"He lives inside the house?" Anna was curious.

"Some of the staff do. They have rooms in a separate wing attached to the house. It's always been that way."

"Sounds feudal," Julie remarked.

"The Gardiner estate was built by Edward's grandfather over seventy years ago." Gino shrugged. "They must have had a dozen workers at the time."

"Who else?" Anna prompted. "Does Alison live there

too?"

"Alison and Sharon both do," Gino replied.

"So that's Edward, Pearson, Alison and Sharon," Anna counted. "Unless you suspect the butler, things don't look good for the women."

"Didn't you say the old man was strangled?" Mary asked. "Wouldn't it require a lot of strength?"

"He suffocated," Anna nodded. "Neither Sharon nor Alison appear delicate to me."

"I almost forgot." Gino wrote something down on his notepad. "The son-in-law, or rather grandson-in-law. Finn O'Malley lives in a small cottage on the property. He must have free access to the main house."

"Who's this guy?" Julie wanted to know.

"Ruth's husband," Mary piped up. "Poor man. He's had more than his share of misfortune."

"O'Malley's a war veteran," Gino supplied. "Almost lost his life in the line of duty."

"What's he doing in Dolphin Bay?" Anna asked. "Is he from around here?"

"I don't think so." Gino frowned. "He was looking for a quiet place to recuperate. Edward invited him here."

"And he never left?" Anna scoffed. "I'd say he outlived his welcome."

"Edward was a generous man." Gino defended his friend. "He liked to have people around him. He insisted Finn make his home here."

"Do you know him well, Gino?"

"I met him a few times." Gino shrugged. "He doesn't talk much. Spends most of his time roaming around the grounds with his dog or fishing in a creek at the far end of the property."

Anna remembered how attached Craig Rose was to the man. She wondered if Finn O'Malley returned his affection.

"Do you know how long Edward had been dead when they found him?" Anna asked Gino. "Did you, err, see him that day?"

"I didn't get a chance." Gino sighed heavily. "They had already taken him away by the time I reached there. I need to tap some of my sources. Maybe Leo or Teddy Fowler will tell us about the time of death."

"Are you meeting Rory Cunningham anytime soon?" Anna asked Mary.

Rory was the medical examiner and a friend of Mary's husband.

"He's coming to our place for the weekly poker game tonight," Mary confirmed. "I better start making that banana cream pie he loves."

"I think we should begin meeting Edward's family, Anna,"

Gino suggested. "Start establishing their alibis."

"Why don't we go there tomorrow? Meg's not here and there's the tree lighting ceremony tonight. We can't miss that."

Gino agreed with Anna.

"I almost forgot about my shopping list. Can't keep your mother waiting."

The women exchanged smiles.

"Don't let her run you ragged, Gino."

"I'm enjoying myself, Anna. Sofia's promised to teach me the perfect risotto. That's one dish I have never been able to get right."

"Mom's never shared that recipe with anyone." Anna was amazed. "You must have made a good first impression."

"I aim to please." Gino stood up and gave them all a mock bow. "Good day, ladies."

"He's a keeper!" Julie trilled as soon as Gino stepped out of the café. "I hope you know that, Anna. What are you doing to keep him happy?"

"You make her sound like his concubine," Mary said, making Anna turn red.

"No, seriously Anna," Julie pressed. "When was the last time you two went on a date?"

"I don't have time for this now, Julie. Why don't we talk about something more important? Like decorating the café and the bookstore."

"She's right." Mary supported Anna. "Have you been outside today? Volunteers are busy decorating the town square. There are wreaths and pretty red bows on all the lamp posts. The gazebo is being decked out in holly and mistletoe. And don't forget the Seaside Christmas Lights contest. We are meeting tonight after the tree lighting ceremony to appoint different group leaders and assign tasks."

"Okay, okay." Julie held up her hand. "I'm not the Grinch here. I already ordered two custom wreaths, Anna. Young stay at home mom a couple of towns over sells them online. I saw them on Instagram. You won't believe how beautiful they are."

"Insta ... what?" Anna made a face. "Is that the new fangled thing Meg keeps talking about?"

"You're a business owner, Anna." Julie rolled her eyes. "You need to step into the new decade and embrace technology."

"What if this young mother of yours fails to deliver? Should I place a backup order somewhere?"

Julie's phone dinged just as she opened her mouth to protest. She tapped her screen and held it up jubilantly.

"That's her. She says she'll be done tomorrow. We can go

pick up the wreaths after lunch."

"I'm not holding my breath," Anna muttered.

"Ye of little faith," Julie sighed. "You're going to love them. Just wait and see."

"I'll make you a whole pan of tiramisu if we come back with the wreaths tomorrow."

Meg swept into the café, her cheeks pink from the cold wind outside.

"Did someone mention tiramisu?"

Chapter 7

The old Mercedes made its way down the winding drive that led to the Gardiner mansion.

"Thanks for coming with me, Cassie." Anna smiled at her daughter. "You know how Julie is when she has a deadline."

"I don't mind, Mom. This is much better than being in the bookstore for hours every day. I don't know how you managed it all these years."

"I love books." Anna shrugged. "And it was my career, just like acting was yours."

"Don't use the past tense yet," Cassie sighed. "This new script I'm reading has a lot of potential."

"Will you have to go to Los Angeles for an audition again?" Anna was curious. "Please don't do it around the holidays. I have my hands full with your Nana. You better stick around for moral support."

"I'm not going anywhere." Cassie parked the car in the ample space before the grand front door. "They might have a video audition. I can do it right from our living room."

"Huh." Anna snorted, expressing what she thought of the idea.

She stepped out of the car and noted the holiday decorations that had adorned the mansion for the big party were still up. She wondered if they should have been taken down.

The door opened and Pearson stood there, his face devoid of any expression.

"Hello there," Anna called out.

She hadn't rehearsed what her story was going to be.

"Ms. Sharon is expecting you." Pearson bowed and started walking down the big foyer.

"Gino must have called Sharon," Cassie observed.

Sharon Gardiner sat in a plush chair, wearing a designer frock that made her look ten years younger. Anna realized she had no idea how old Sharon really was. The cherry sized rubies she wore in her ears sparkled as they caught the wintery sunlight streaming through the tall bay windows.

"Hello, hello." Sharon leapt up and greeted them with a smile. "It's nice of you to come. I thought Gino would be here too."

"He's meeting some suppliers," Anna fibbed. "The vineyard keeps him busy."

"He's a workaholic, just like my brother. That's why they always got along well. Edward thinks the world of him, you know."

Sharon had dispatched the butler to get some refreshments.

He arrived with a tray loaded with a wide assortment of cookies and glasses of chilled eggnog.

"We always serve eggnog during the holidays," Sharon laughed. "It's a family recipe handed down since my grandpa's time."

Anna found Sharon's exuberance puzzling. She couldn't decide if the woman was touched in the head or just nervous. She gave no outward appearance of grief. Maybe she hadn't been close to her brother.

"Your brother was a lot older than you, Sharon," Anna remarked.

"Edward was more like a father figure," Sharon nodded, daintily nibbling on a sugar cookie. "He was almost thirty when I was born. I was three when he got married to his Beth. They say I was the cutest flower girl in the family."

Anna tried to calculate how old Edward's mother must have been when she had Sharon.

"Our father remarried." Sharon answered her question. "Edward's mother died when he was in college. Dad mourned her for several years. I don't think anyone expected him to bring home a second wife."

Anna tried to hide her surprise. She wondered if Gino knew Sharon was Edward's half sister.

"My parents died when I was barely in my teens," Sharon continued. "Edward was such a dear. He never let me feel they were gone."

Anna extended her apologies.

"No worries." Sharon played with a ring she wore on her right hand. "Premature death seems to be a thing in our family. Edward's mom, then my parents, Edward's son, his daughter ... they were all taken from us too soon."

"I wonder how you cope with it," Cassie said sincerely. "We're still trying to come to terms with my father's death."

"Did your brother have any ailments? Any chronic health conditions?" Anna decided it was time to ask some pertinent questions.

"Edward was healthy as a horse. You saw him yourself that night at the party."

"He was quite spry for someone his age," Anna agreed. "Did he get into an argument with anyone recently?"

"Edward never argued." Sharon started pacing around the room. "He was friendly with everyone. He believed money combined with a kind word solved most problems. And he had plenty of both to spread around."

"So he didn't get any threatening notes or phone calls?"

"Not to my knowledge." Sharon looked thoughtful. "Knowing Edward, he would have kept anything unpleasant to himself. He was very protective of us, you know. Just wanted us to be happy and have a good time."

Anna had no doubt Sharon was doing just that. She noted the large stockings hanging over the fireplace and read the names off them in her mind.

"You have two extra stockings," she murmured, then realized she had spoken out loud.

"Oh that!" Sharon giggled. "Probably for some new kid Edward's taken under his wing."

"How do you mean?" Anna was puzzled.

"Some protégé or charity case," Sharon dismissed. "Edward championed a lot of causes. He said he was making up for all the kids he didn't have."

"Sounds like a true philanthropist." Cassie's eyes shone with admiration. "Most Hollywood people I know do it for the photo op."

"My Edward wasn't like that." Sharon's face fell for a split second. "He was the real McCoy. Had a heart of gold."

Anna didn't know what to believe. Despite the rosy picture Sharon painted, someone had attacked the poor old man in the middle of the night and wrung the life out of him.

"Can we get a tour of the house?" Anna asked. "I want to get an idea of the general layout."

"Of course!" Sharon pressed a discreet button next to the fireplace. "Pearson can show you around. You will have to excuse me now, though. I'm going up to San Francisco for some holiday shopping."

The butler appeared beside them and nodded at Sharon's

instructions. She picked up her bag and sailed out of the door, waving goodbye to the Butlers.

"That's a genuine Birkin," Cassie whispered to Anna. "Do you know how hard they are to come by?"

"Miss Sharon collects those bags," Pearson said fondly. "My master bought a dozen of them for her birthday one year, in twelve of their best colors."

Cassie's eyes popped out of their sockets. Anna realized the Gardiners had more money than she could ever imagine.

Pearson spoke in a dull monotone as he took them around the house. After going through an opulent parlor and sitting room, they entered a dining room that could seat a dozen. Anna fell in love with the library that spanned the length of the entire first floor. She noted the door that led into the backyard from the kitchen.

"Is that the only way in other than the front door?" she asked Pearson.

"There's a hidden door in the library," the butler informed her. "Mr. O'Malley uses it a lot. And the French windows in the family room open onto a terrace. I guess it would be easy to come in that way."

"Where are your rooms?" Anna asked. "You live in this house too, don't you?"

"In a manner of speaking," he replied, opening a green door that led to a covered passage.

Anna and Cassie followed him down the long carpeted

hallway to a small foyer. There was a cozy living room with a fireplace and big television. Another passage led to four doors.

"How many people live here, Pearson, other than you?" Anna inquired.

"The cook and the maid," he offered. "One of the rooms is empty at the moment."

"Is that green door locked at night?" Anna asked, knowing she wasn't being very subtle.

Pearson shook his head.

"The cook has been here for over thirty years. Martha, the maid, is her niece. She started working here when she was sixteen. Neither of them would dream of harming the master."

They went back into the main house and climbed the big staircase to the second floor. Half of it was occupied by the ballroom where the holiday party had been held. The other half was split into two large suites belonging to Edward and his sister Sharon.

"You must know everything that goes on in this house, Pearson." Anna decided a little flattery wouldn't hurt.

"It would be unethical to violate the family's privacy." Pearson's voice dripped with contempt. "And it's against the code of conduct I adhere to, Madam."

"You do remember your master has been murdered?"

"You're an outsider," Cassie told him. "You will be the first person the police suspect."

"I would never harm Mr. Gardiner!" Pearson looked shocked. "Just the very idea is ridiculous."

"Tell us who would," Anna stepped in. "Who do you think might have wanted to hurt your boss."

Pearson didn't hesitate.

"Mr. O'Malley. I never trusted him."

"Why is that?" Cassie asked.

"He's a mean drunk. Gets into a tizzy and goes on and on about how the old man doesn't treat him right. Says he was set aside after little Ruth died. He's living here, isn't he? Eating at my master's table? He has no right to go around bad mouthing him. No right."

Anna was surprised to see Pearson so disturbed. It was the first time he had displayed any emotion.

The tour ended prematurely when Anna realized how late it was. They thanked Pearson and showed themselves out.

On the drive back, Anna tried to process what she had learned while Cassie chattered about the latest texts from Bobby.

"I told him he better get here by Christmas. Do you think we have enough room for him, Mom? We can put an air mattress in my room. He won't mind."

"Bobby's always welcome, dear," Anna replied absently.

The café was bustling when they got back and Meg was looking stressed.

"We're back!" Cassie exclaimed. "Anything interesting happen today, Meg?"

"I'll say!" Meg shook her head. "You know that jerk from DBU? He actually came in here."

"What did he want?" Anna asked worriedly. "You didn't get into a fight, did you?"

"I never got the chance," Meg smirked. "He ordered a cup of coffee and started talking about how I had impressed him the other day. Said I was a born crusader and he couldn't wait for me to join their cause."

"I think he's sweet on you," Cassie giggled. "Did you at least get a good look at him this time?"

Meg blushed.

"He's not bad looking," she admitted grudgingly. "Could use a haircut though. And a shower."

"Is he conserving water by not taking a bath?" Anna was aghast. "Meg, I think you should stay away from this boy."

"He came looking for me, Anna!" Meg fumed.

She flung her apron off and told them she was taking a break. Anna and Cassie stared wide eyed as Meg stalked into the bookstore through the connecting arch.

"Did you see that, Mom?" Cassie chortled. "I think she likes this kid."

Chapter 8

Anna tore the basil leaves she had picked from her garden and sprinkled them over the hot casserole she had just pulled out of the oven.

Cassie uncorked two bottles of Mystic Hill wine while Meg set the table. Sofia stood like a martinet, hands on her hips, ordering them about.

Gino and his nephew were coming to dinner and Sofia had insisted Anna pull out the good china.

"But we only use it for special days," Anna protested.

"It's the holidays, Anna, and you have a handsome, eligible Italian man coming to dinner. I'm thinking about your future here."

"You'll embarrass him." Anna was worried.

"Italian men appreciate good food," Sofia stated.

The doorbell rang and Cassie rushed to get it. Anna heard Gino's deep voice and couldn't resist a smile.

The group sat in the living room, noshing on the magnificent cheese and charcuterie tray Sofia had put together.

"Did you talk to Teddy Fowler?" Anna asked Gino. She turned to Leo. "I don't suppose you are working on this case?"

Leo told them he was assisting Teddy but couldn't talk about an ongoing investigation.

"Don't worry," Cassie assured him. "We can usually get all the information we want from Teddy. We won't be pestering you."

Leo looked relieved.

"I spoke to some of my old buddies," Gino volunteered. "The police are trying to establish a motive. The general consensus is that Edward was killed for his money."

"That seems obvious, given how rich the man was," Sofia offered. "A little too obvious, I'd say."

"What do you think, Nana?" Cassie's eyes gleamed with mischief. "Was it a crime of passion?"

"Was it a scorned lover?" Meg joined in.

"Stop it, you two." Anna tried to hide a smile.

Sofia declared it was time to serve the main meal. Gino exclaimed in Italian when he saw the loaded table and gave Sofia a tight hug. He carved the roast chicken on Anna's request.

Sofia cut generous slices of her Italian sausage lasagna and insisted on serving everyone herself. Meg passed around the tomato and cucumber salad studded with fat olives and pickled peppers. It had been a regular item at the dinner table since Sofia arrived.

"How was your trip to the Gardiner estate?" Gino asked Anna. "Did you learn anything new?"

"It was quite uneventful."

Anna told Gino about Sharon.

"I can't make up my mind about her. Is she a bit whacko or just insensitive? How could she go shopping to the city mere days after she lost her brother?"

"People cope in different ways, Anna." Gino took a hearty bite of the lasagna and asked Leo to pass him the roasted vegetables.

"I think it's extremely selfish of her," Anna huffed.

"What's the matter?" Sofia intruded. "You don't like my lasagna? Why are you pushing food around your plate?"

"The lasagna's delicious, Mama," Anna soothed. "Just a bit rich for me."

"You're not feeling queasy, are you, Mom?" Cassie's voice was laced with concern. "Do you want that nausea medicine the doctor asked you to keep on hand?"

"That was just during the ch…" Anna stopped mid sentence.

She widened her eyes at Cassie, hoping she would take the

hint and change the topic.

"What is going on here?" Sofia demanded. "Anna, are you suffering from dyspepsia?" She turned to Meg. "Go to my room and get the bottle of Pepto. It will set her right in no time."

"Okay, Mama." Anna hung her head.

Gino was giving Anna some concerned looks.

"Did you know Sharon was Edward's half sister?" Cassie asked Gino. "I would never have guessed that, given how similar they look."

"The dimple in the left cheek and the green eyes are classic Gardiner traits," Gino told them. "Edward's father and grandfather looked the same. Edward loved Sharon like a daughter. They became especially close after he lost his son."

"And she never married?" Anna asked. "She's an attractive woman, Gino. I'm sure she had plenty of suitors."

"Don't forget the money, Mom." Cassie sighed dramatically. "If I were a man, I wouldn't have cared how she looked."

"She was quite reckless in her youth," Gino told them. "Their parents had passed on and Edward indulged her every whim."

"He didn't have any eligible friends?" Anna wondered out loud. "I guess they would've been much older."

"Did she have access to the money?" Cassie asked. "She must have some stake in the family wealth, considering there were only two of them."

"We never talked about that," Gino shrugged. "That's a good point, Cassie."

"She must be dependent on Edward in some way though," Anna argued. "Why else would she stay in the same house with her half brother?"

"Didn't you say this Edward was like a father to her?" Sofia frowned. "What's wrong with living with your own family?"

"Says the woman who moved hundreds of miles away from hers," Anna shot back.

"What's for dessert, Nana?" Meg sat back, holding her stomach. "I barely have room for anything more."

"Cannoli," Sofia smiled indulgently. "And chocolate gelato. Cassie told me you like chocolate."

"What do you think about Pearson?" Anna asked Gino. "Do you trust him?"

"He's loyal to a fault."

"Pearson said Edward was excited about some announcement he was going to make at Christmas."

"He couldn't stop talking about it at the party. Don't you remember, Anna?"

"Any idea what it might have been?"

"Knowing Edward, it was probably a big donation to some charity." Gino put his fork down. "I can't eat a bite more. Thank you for a wonderful meal, Sofia. Can you teach me how to make this lasagna?"

The doorbell rang, announcing a new arrival.

"That must be Julie." Anna stood up. "She's joining us for dessert."

Meg followed Sofia into the kitchen. She came back with a stack of dessert plates. Sofia was right behind, holding a large platter of homemade cannoli.

"I'm starving!" Julie swept into the room, dressed in a colorful plaid shirt and capris. "Wrote all day without breaking for lunch."

Sofia started fixing her a plate.

Julie alternated between big bites of chicken and lasagna and didn't come up for air until she had mopped up the last bit of sauce with a piece of crusty bread.

"Has Mary talked to you about the Seaside Christmas Lights stuff, Meg?" she asked. "They are meeting at the town hall tonight."

"I forgot all about that!" Meg paused while scooping the gelato. "What time is it?"

"I'm going there myself, Meg." Leo smiled. "You can join me if you like."

"There's plenty of time," Julie assured her. "They don't meet until 8 PM."

"Mary didn't say why she wants me there, Anna." Meg's eyes were huge. "I have never been to a town meeting."

"Leo's going with you," Anna reminded her. "And you will know most people there."

"Sally Davis and Mary are heading the Lights Committee this year." Julie held a cannoli bursting with sweet cream. "What are you worried about?"

"When are we getting our tree, Mom?" Cassie asked. "Do you even know where we are going?"

"There's a Christmas tree lot five miles north on the coastal highway," Gino spoke up. "Leo and I are planning to go pick our tree tomorrow. Why don't you all join us?"

"Great idea!" Sofia sprang up. "We can take thermoses of hot chocolate and I can make my special giardiniera sandwiches. That farm boy Cassie used to date dropped off some nice grapes today."

"Please," Anna pleaded. "No more talk about food. I'm bursting at the seams here."

"We need to eat," Sofia reasoned. "Picking a Christmas tree can be very exhausting. And we are choosing at least four."

"I'm not getting a separate tree," Julie groaned. "Yours will be enough for me."

"Nonsense!" Sofia ordered. "We are doing Christmas right this year. You've let things slide in my absence."

"What about a tree for the café?" Anna felt dazed. "John and I always got a tree for the bookstore."

"Get two," Gino said. "One for the bookstore and one for the café."

"What if we ask people to donate?" Meg asked shyly. "We can ask them to place their gifts under the tree, then take them to some children's home two days before Christmas."

"That's a wonderful idea!" Anna said brightly and Sofia clapped her hands in approval.

"I second that, Meg." Leo gave her an admiring look.

"So how many trees does that make?" Gino laughed. "Even with my 4x4, we'll need multiple trips."

"I'll have to close the café early, if all of us want to go." Anna wondered when she would get a chance to meet Finn O'Malley.

Chapter 9

Anna cupped her hands around a steaming mug of coffee and gently blew on it. She couldn't stop smiling. Julie and Mary, her best friends, sat before her, dressed in matching red holiday sweaters. Mary had knit them for the Firecrackers fifteen years ago and that had started a tradition. They always wore them when they went to pick a Christmas tree. Anna was surprised the old sweater still fit her.

Sofia sat on Anna's left, pouring over some list she had made. Cassie sat on her other side, tapping some keys on her phone. Meg stood behind her with her hands on Anna's shoulders.

They were all waiting for Gino and Leo to join them.

Anna hadn't been this happy in a long time. She wanted to lock this moment in her memory so she could cherish it on long winter nights when her little birdies flew the coop.

"We need at least six trees." Sofia looked up from her list. "We should be able to wrangle a big discount. And we need thousands of fairy lights, Anna."

"There's plenty of old lights in the basement, Mama."

"You need to buy some new lights for the store." Julie looked around. "You can't string those old mismatched lights in here, Anna. The storefront needs a theme. I've already made a rough design. It matches the wreaths."

Julie's contact had delivered the handmade wreaths as promised. They were so huge Anna could barely hold them herself. The customers couldn't stop talking about how beautiful they were and wanted to know where Anna found them. She had finally pinned a paper with the girl's contact details up on the bulletin board.

"What's keeping Gino?" Sofia grumbled. "I want to get there before it gets dark."

Dolphin Bay was experiencing a misty day with intermittent showers. The mercury had dipped below fifty, spurring people to bundle up.

"How was your dinner at the Yellow Tulip?" Julie asked Mary.

"I was glad to get a break from cooking." Mary's husband notoriously hated eating out. She didn't mind because she loved to cook for him. Lately, she had begun to crave a change. Their daughter had intervened, suggesting they have a 'date night' once a month.

"You went there again?" Anna grimaced.

"The only other restaurant is the China Garden." Mary shrugged. "You know my Ben isn't fond of Chinese food."

"When is Ben taking you to a nice place for date night?" Julie pounced. "That tight fisted miser! You need to put your foot down, Mary. You can be too docile."

"I didn't want to drive too far in this weather. At least you can be sure of a hearty meal when you go to the Yellow Tulip."

"That's true," Anna agreed. "So? Do they have a special menu for the holidays?"

"They do." Mary added sugar to her coffee. "But it doesn't start until a week before Christmas. We got the special of the day, rosemary crusted lamb with roasted potatoes and creamed spinach. They had cherry bread pudding for dessert."

"Never heard of that," Sofia dismissed. "What's wrong with cannoli or tiramisu?"

"It's a diner, Mama, not an Italian restaurant."

"There's one thing at the Yellow Tulip that's tastier than the food." Julie had a naughty gleam in her eye. "Spill it, Mary!"

"What are you talking about, Aunt Julie?" Cassie asked.

"Gossip, of course." Julie poked Mary in the arm. "What's the latest in Dolphin Bay? Come on, Mary. Give us the scoop."

"Was anyone talking about the murder?" Anna asked.

Mary set her coffee cup down.

"That does seem to be the topic of the week. You know how it is, Anna. People are ghouls."

"Can't blame them, Mary." Anna stifled a yawn. "I don't think anyone expected something tragic like this to happen to the Gardiners."

"So what's the word on the street?" Julie was impatient. "Who done it?"

"It's not as simple as that, Julie," Anna protested.

"Public opinion rarely has any rhyme or reason," Cassie said. "The press has hung me up to dry many a time, with no fault of mine."

"People actually don't have a clue about what happened," Mary told them. "Some are saying Edward was shot in broad daylight. Others say he was poisoned."

"That's ridiculous!" Meg stepped in. "The Chronicle reported the whole story. People should at least know the poor old man died in his sleep."

"The truth has a way of getting twisted, dear." Anna kissed Meg's hand. "Don't lose your cool over this."

"Most people are blaming the butler," Mary continued.

"Pearson?" Anna leaned forward. "Are they saying why?"

"Pearson goes to the Tipsy Whale every week on his night off. He enjoys his whiskey, it seems. He's been grumbling about his employer after a couple of drinks." Mary sucked in a breath. "He talked about pushing Edward down the stairs!"

"Wow!" Julie grinned. "And you were sitting on it all this

time? You're a sly one, Mary."

"Wait a minute," Anna interrupted. "That's just drunken nonsense. That doesn't mean he really did it."

"And Mr. Gardiner didn't actually fall down the stairs," Meg reminded them.

"This group of old biddies said he looks like a killer."

"Even I can tell you that's ridiculous!" Sofia had abandoned her list and started listening in.

Anna thought of Pearson with his respectful manner and middle aged paunch. His knees had creaked when they climbed up the staircase to the second floor. Anna had thought he was exceptionally protective of all the Gardiners.

"You wanted to know the gossip." Mary looked worried. She hated disagreements and avoided them at all costs.

Anna felt a draft of cold air and craned her neck to see who had entered the café. Gino rushed toward their table, looking apologetic. Leo was right behind him.

"I'm sorry, ladies. There was a last minute crisis at the winery. But I'm all yours now."

"I'm off duty too." Leo beamed at Meg.

"I guess we'll have to skip lunch." Julie winked at Cassie. "We're too late already, right, Sofia?"

"There's a picnic basket full of food in your car, Julie." Sofia rolled her eyes. "We can stop for a quick meal somewhere."

"I know just the place." Gino rubbed his hands. "There's a scenic outlook on the coastal highway two miles out of town. Pretty spot in a wooded area with some picnic benches. The land slopes down to the cliffs and you can see the ocean in the distance. Wildflowers grow there in the spring. It's beautiful!"

"So we will have a picnic lunch!" Sofia declared. "Let's get going."

Gino's housekeeper had provided fried chicken and corn muffins. Sofia had brought three kinds of sandwiches with salami, fresh mozzarella and ham along with a macaroni salad loaded with olives and sweet peppers.

It was a day to remember. The group ate every morsel of food and Sofia surprised everyone by taking pictures with her phone. She sent them to her friends at the senior community. Anna was particularly touched when Sofia posed with an arm around Meg, bursting with pride and happiness.

They spent three hours at the Christmas tree farm, going back and forth over the right choice. Finally, they selected six firs based on everyone's likes and preferences.

"Any update on that script?" Anna asked Cassie as they stood in line, sipping hot chocolate.

Sofia and Meg were selecting yard decorations.

"I gave a video audition. They are going to get back to me after the holidays. That means I didn't get the role, Mom."

"Don't give up yet, Cassie." Anna tried to be supportive without being critical. "You've been away for a long time."

"I'm not thinking about it right now." Cassie was unperturbed. "I am going to enjoy the holidays and get to know Meg better."

"Has she said anything more about that boy?" Anna deftly changed the subject.

Cassie shook her head. "She talked to a counselor about her gap year. They see a lot of kids doing that nowadays, it seems. Her SAT scores are high and she has good grades. She's moved around so much though. They told her to address it in her essay."

"Does she really want to go to DBU though?" Anna couldn't hide the hope in her voice. "I don't want to hold her back."

"She knows that, Mom. We talked about it. Meg never thought she would go to college. She said the only thing she ever dreamt about was reconnecting with her birth parents."

Anna felt her eyes grow moist.

"And we are lucky that dream came true. But she needs bigger dreams now. It's our job to encourage her, Cassie."

"I totally agree, Mom." Cassie wove her arm around

Anna's. "I told her the same thing. She can go study art in Europe if she wants to. I'll take a TV gig if I have to, or sell some of my baubles. I don't have much use for them in Dolphin Bay anyway."

Anna swallowed a lump and marveled at how much Cassie had matured in the past few months. Meg's arrival had affected all of them.

"Isn't that Alison Gardiner?" Meg whispered in Anna's ear, subtly pointing toward a tall, green eyed girl strolling hand in hand with a dark haired young man. "What is she doing here?"

Chapter 10

Cassie chatted with Mrs. Chang, the proprietor of the China Garden restaurant. She was picking up dinner. After a massive cooking spree that had lasted for some days, Sofia had finally admitted she could use a break. No one wanted to admit they craved something different after a week of Italian food.

"Are you sure you added two orders of orange chicken?" she asked the woman. "And the crab wontons and spring rolls?"

Mrs. Chang bobbed her head and leaned forward conspiratorially.

"Who is Anna's top suspect?"

Cassie mentally rolled her eyes. She figured the whole town knew by now that Anna was looking into Edward's death.

"I have no idea. Why don't you ask her, Mrs. Chang?"

"I say it is that man who doesn't talk. You know, the one who goes everywhere with his dog?"

Cassie's eyes widened.

"You mean Finn O'Malley?"

The man was as grumpy as they came. Anna and Cassie had encountered him when they had gone to the Gardiner mansion the first time. He had been lurking around their car, a big German Shepherd at his heels. He turned his back on them when they spotted him. Anna had called out a greeting but there was no response. Pearson told them the man didn't talk much. He was the same with everyone.

"He hated the old man," Mrs. Chang supplied. "Blamed him for his wife's death. I think he took revenge."

Cassie tried to process what she had heard.

"Finn thought Mr. Gardiner was responsible for Ruth's death? That doesn't make sense. Why would he harm his granddaughter?"

"He was careless." Mrs. Chang shrugged. "Man thinks old man did not pay attention to Ruth. She and baby both died."

Cassie couldn't believe a man like Edward Gardiner had been negligent toward his own granddaughter.

"How do you know this, Mrs. Chang?"

"My nephew goes to support group …"

She didn't elaborate further. Cassie didn't want to know who had violated Finn's privacy.

"Thanks, Mrs. Chang! The food smells good. You didn't forget the fortune cookies, did you?"

Cassie hefted the two bags bursting with steaming cartons

of food and started walking home. She couldn't wait to tell Anna what she had just learnt.

The Butler house was the brightest house on the street. Tiny festive wreaths hung in the windows and lights were strung on every available surface. A nativity scene took up one side of the front lawn while some reindeer reposed on the other.

Cassie went in and stopped to stare at the tree in the foyer. They were still decorating it. Anna had been digging out box after box of ornaments from the attic and the garage. Red and gold orbs hung on the branches, dragging them down with their weight. Crystal snowflakes were interspersed in between. A gold ribbon was draped around the tree from top to bottom. They were going to make popcorn garlands next.

"We're in the dining room, Cassie," Anna called out.

"What took you so long, girl?" Sofia sipped wine and glowered at her.

"You'll never believe this!" Cassie dumped the bag of takeout on the table and started telling Anna about her conversation with Mrs. Chang.

"So Finn had a grudge against Edward?" Anna's eyebrows shot up. "That changes things. We need to find out more about this."

"Have you seen the stockings, Cassie?" Meg asked eagerly. "We just hung them over the fireplace."

She almost dragged Cassie into the living room.

Sofia muttered disapprovingly and started munching on a spring roll.

"Why don't we start, Mama?" Anna suggested. "The girls will join us."

Cassie and Meg heard her and trooped back to the dining room. Everyone was hungry and they devoted themselves to doing justice to the food.

Meg stood up as soon as she was done.

"I have to go to the town hall for a meeting. All the Seaside Lights volunteers are going to get their tasks assigned tonight."

"But Cassie's making her famous banana fritters," Anna reminded her. "Are you going to miss dessert?"

"Save some for me, please?" Meg pleaded. "I want to get there early. Otherwise I'll be stuck with the jobs nobody wants."

"Sit down, young lady!" Sofia put her fork down. "What about the popcorn garlands? Everyone in the family is involved in making those. It's tradition."

Meg looked torn.

"Can we do that after I get back, Nana?"

"Let her go, Nana," Cassie pleaded. "We can sit by the fire, sip some wine and catch up. Tell me about your friends down south."

Sofia capitulated with a smile. "Don't forget your coat. We'll wait for you."

They decided to postpone dessert until Meg got back.

Cassie topped up their wine and took the glasses out to the living room. She curled up in her favorite chair and gazed at the jumbo red stockings with everyone's names on them. She couldn't stop looking at them.

"This is nice, isn't it, Mom?" she sighed. "I'd forgotten what Christmas at home feels like."

"We missed you a lot, you know." Anna's eyes misted. "Your father and I couldn't stop wishing you would surprise us with a visit. We had the foster kids some years, but there were times when it was just the two of us."

"I wanted to be here, Mom." Cassie was apologetic. "No matter where I was in the world, I wanted to be right here in this living room. I was thinking about you, and believe it or not, I was thinking about Meg."

"We're all here now." Anna smiled. "That's what matters most, Cassie."

"If only we didn't have these distractions. Seriously, Mom, why are you getting involved in this Gardiner business? We hardly knew the man."

"Your grandpa worked for him all his life, Cassie." Sofia looked grim. "He looked up to the man. Edward always took care of us. Now it's our turn. Anna should help if she can."

"I was just helping Gino. You know how he supported me against Lara Crawford. But Mom's right too."

Cassie saw Anna's eyelid twitch and wondered why her mother seemed nervous. Was she hiding something?

"Okay Mom. But can't you do this after the holidays? Why spoil the Christmas cheer?"

"I was thinking the same thing," Anna admitted. "But life doesn't always follow our agenda."

"What does that mean?" Sofia asked.

"One of my old customers came into the bookstore today. She's about your age, Cassie. Martha Collins. Do you know her?"

"Does she look over her shoulder a lot?" Cassie asked. "I think I remember her from high school. She was really short and pudgy."

"She's still the same," Anna laughed. "And she wheezes every now and then. Martha's fond of romance books. She buys one at the beginning of every month."

"What about this girl?" Sofia was impatient. "Stop blabbering and get to the point, Anna."

"Sorry Mama. Anyway, it turns out Martha works as a maid at the Gardiner mansion. She's been living there all these years and I never knew."

"She must be the cook's niece Pearson was telling us about," Cassie reminded her.

"Martha seems very fond of Sharon and Alison. She told me Edward didn't like Finn O'Malley. The two barely spoke to each other."

"That doesn't make sense," Sofia said. "You say this grandson-in-law lives with the family. Why would Edward take him in if he resented him?"

"Finn doesn't actually live in the main house, Nana," Cassie explained. "He lives in a small cottage on the property. They could go days without seeing each other."

"Not true, Cassie. Pearson said Finn ate with the family."

"Is that all Martha said, Mom?"

Anna's eyes gleamed with excitement.

"That's just it. She told me Edward and Finn had a big fight the day after the Christmas party. That's what, a couple of days before the old man died, right?"

"Did she say what the fight was about?" Cassie's eyes widened.

"She doesn't know. They were in the library. Martha said she heard raised voices but couldn't tell what they were saying. Sharon had to intervene, apparently."

"You have your work cut out for you, Mom. You need to talk to both Sharon and Finn O'Malley. Just promise you won't go there alone."

"I wish it were that simple. Finn barely says a word and Sharon talks too much. Getting either of them to say something pertinent is going to be a challenge."

Cassie's brain was off on a different track.

"Did Gino know Sharon back in the day?"

"What are you hinting at, Cassie?"

"It seems natural that Gino and Sharon would have moved in the same circles when they were young. So it's not a stretch to think they might have dated at some point."

"So what? That was a long time ago."

"Don't you see, Mom? They live in the same town and they are both single. How do you know he's not still seeing her?"

Chapter 11

Anna packed two cranberry sage cupcakes in the fancy new boxes with the café logo. Cassie said they would help spread the word about Anna's Café. Then she had given Anna a long spiel about how branding was necessary for any business. Meg had designed the simple logo with Anna's Café in a cursive font with two magnolia flowers on either side.

"I hear you are looking into Edward Gardiner's death, Anna." Ian Samuels picked up his cupcakes and coffee. "Any progress so far?"

"You probably know more about it than I do, Ian," Anna joked. "I'm thinking of sitting down with you to swap notes."

"You know where I am all day. Come down to the Chronicle any time."

Anna waved goodbye and reluctantly glanced at the corner table. The short, frail man sitting there nursed his coffee and gave Anna a piercing look. She couldn't ignore him any longer.

Anna poured a cup of coffee for herself and walked over.

"Why are you here?" she asked Craig Rose.

"I want an update." His tone was harsh. "What steps have you taken to prove Finn's innocence?"

"I never promised you that. I'm just going to figure out what happened to Edward. Or I'm going to try."

"You do want to know what your husband was keeping from you?"

Anna tried to hide her desperation.

"How do I know you're not bluffing?"

"You don't. I'm calling the shots here."

Craig Rose stood up and walked out without another word.

The Firecrackers arrived for coffee. Cassie came in through the bookstore.

"Have you started shopping for presents, Aunt Julie?" she winked.

"Are we giving presents?" Julie looked shocked.

"Well, duh!" Mary gave her a frown. "It's Christmas, Julie. Of course we are getting presents for each other."

"This is the first year Meg's with us," Anna said brightly. "And Cassie's home after a long time."

"Don't forget the main thing, Mom." Cassie hugged her mother. "You are cancer free."

"At least for now," Anna murmured.

"It's a special year," Mary nodded. "You think we should make a shopping trip to the city?"

They plunged into a lively discussion about which malls to visit and whether to share a wish list or not.

"Look at the time." Anna sprang up. "I'm late for lunch with Gino."

"You're wearing that on a date?" Cassie crinkled her eyes at Anna's outfit of dark trousers and pine green cable knit sweater.

"What's wrong with this?" Anna gave herself a quick onceover. "And it's not a date. It's just a working lunch."

"Doesn't hurt to look your best," Julie offered.

"Just a little spruce up won't hurt," Mary added.

Cassie pulled out a tube of lipstick from the pocket of her jeans. It was dark red.

"Chanel always works. This shade is perfect for the season."

Anna protested. She never wore dark lipstick. The girls prevailed and sent her off feeling a bit self conscious.

Gino was meeting her at the Yellow Tulip. He was already seated in a booth when Anna reached the diner. His face lit up when he spotted her.

"You look pretty today, Anna." He stood up to help her in.

Anna thanked him blushingly and hid behind the menu she knew by heart.

They both ordered ham and cheese sandwiches with a side of onion rings.

"Things don't look good for O'Malley."

"Did you talk to Teddy Fowler?" Anna looked over her shoulder, hoping the booth behind them was empty.

Rumors spread like wildfire at the Yellow Tulip.

"Their theory is that Edward was killed for his money. Finn O'Malley was dependent on the old man. He is also known to be irascible and impulsive which works against him."

"Didn't he win some kind of medal?" Anna was surprised. "He must get a pension for being a soldier. Why would he depend on Edward?"

"He got used to the good life?" Gino absently picked up his jumbo sandwich and took a hearty bite. "I don't understand why he lives here. His wife is gone and they didn't have any kids."

"You think he was sponging off the old man."

"Makes sense, doesn't it? You were there at the Christmas party. The Gardiners live like that every day, Anna."

"Easy to get used to being waited upon by maids and butlers," Anna agreed. "Didn't Edward's largesse depend on him staying alive, though? What's the guarantee that whoever inherits will allow Finn to stick around?"

"That's a good question. So is what you want for dessert."

Anna laughed and reminded Gino she was surrounded by sweets all day.

"What about that big announcement Edward was going to make?"

"He hinted about it to a lot of people." Gino asked the waitress for a piece of pumpkin pie. "But none of them had an inkling of what was coming."

"My gut instinct says that announcement was important. We need to find out more about it."

Gino left for an appointment soon after, promising he would keep Anna updated. Anna enjoyed the walk back to the café. It was a bright and sunny December morning with salty breezes blowing in from the bay. Anna decided it was just cold enough to be enjoyable. People greeted each other joyously and the holiday spirit was evident everywhere.

Sofia was waiting for her at the café. Anna remembered they were supposed to decorate the trees in the café and bookstore that afternoon. Meg and Cassie pitched in and they had a merry time of it.

Anna had ordered some custom ornaments on the sly. The girls exclaimed when they saw their names engraved on shiny gold orbs. Sofia insisted on taking pictures before they went home.

Dinner was boisterous, although it was just the four of them. Anna was pleased to see everyone happy. Sofia had made a big pot of ribollita, a hearty Tuscan soup with vegetables and greens. Cassie made her special garlic bread. It was a simple but tasty meal. They were all feeling a little worn out and everyone wanted an early night.

Anna finished her daily baking the next morning and rushed through her breakfast. Julie was going to pick her up. They planned to pay George Pearson another visit.

If Pearson was surprised to see them, he didn't show it.

"Ms. Sharon is out meeting some friends."

"We are here to see you, Pearson." Anna smiled encouragingly. "Can we talk somewhere?"

The butler led them to a small room near the kitchen. Anna hadn't noticed it before. Pearson told them he used it as an office.

"So you hang out here all day until you are summoned?" Julie noted heartily.

Two fat bookshelves covered a wall, crammed with all kinds of books. Either Pearson was a voracious reader or he wasn't very discerning. A turntable reposed on a side table next to a stack of vinyl records.

"How can I help you, Madam?" Pearson was deferential.

"I won't beat around the bush," Anna began. "You were heard badmouthing your employer at the pub."

The man looked sheepish.

"That's not all," Anna continued. "You said you were going to push him down the stairs."

"I don't remember that!" Pearson looked alarmed. "I must have been drunk."

"This doesn't look good for you, Pearson. You publicly declared your intention of hurting Edward. What was that about?"

"It was nothing, believe me. I was just frustrated. Do you know I have devoted my life to this family? I've worked here for forty years, since I was a lad of fifteen. Never thought of leaving."

"So this was about money?" Julie prompted.

"I have a good life here. Now. But I need to think of retirement. I wanted Mr. Gardiner to settle something on me right now, while he was still alive."

"He didn't agree?" Anna sympathized.

"He told me he would think about it. I thought he was just brushing me off. So I went to the pub to let off steam."

"Are you sure you didn't take it out on him?" Anna asked grimly.

"There was no need to. Mr. Gardiner called me in two days later and told me about a trust fund he created for me. I would get a generous pension as long as I was alive. He also gave me a big Christmas bonus and a raise."

Pearson looked wistful when he told them about his windfall.

"Mr. Gardiner was generous to a fault. I feel embarrassed about that hissy fit I threw at the Tipsy Whale. I just hope he never knew about it."

Anna and Julie politely declined Pearson's offer of eggnog and headed back to the café.

"What are you thinking?" Julie asked.

"If Edward was this generous to his butler, think what he must have done for his family?"

Julie nodded in agreement.

"He must have made sure they were all comfortable long after he was gone."

Anna sighed.

"So unless someone got really greedy, there was no need to kill him for his money."

Chapter 12

Anna closed her eyes and savored the flavor of the taco she had just eaten.

"These fish tacos are incredible, Mama. Where did you learn how to make these?"

Sofia beamed with pleasure.

"We have a Mexican chef at the senior center. These tacos are his specialty, Anna. They are the most asked for on Taco Tuesday."

"I'm not very familiar with Mexican food." Meg licked some sauce off her fingers. "But I love it. This sauce, Nana. I have never tasted anything like this."

"That's ancho chili salsa, Meg. I had to hound the chef for months to get this recipe. We finally agreed to swap. Had to give him the secret ingredient for my tiramisu."

"Bobby's back," Cassie announced. "He went in shock when we had a video call today. Says I have put on twenty pounds. I told him it's Nana's fault."

"When am I meeting this Bobby?" Sofia pouted. "He has no respect for good food."

"Oh no, Mama," Anna corrected her. "Bobby loves my

cooking. He's a fitness trainer so he can't help commenting on people's weight."

Anna had made a caramel cake for dessert. She topped each slice with a dollop of cinnamon whipped cream.

"Let's talk about the Christmas Eve party now, Mom." Cassie licked her spoon. "Mom and Dad have been throwing this party since I was a child, Meg. Everyone wants an invitation."

"I haven't had the party since your Dad passed." Anna's voice was laced with sadness. "But I think it's time to revive the tradition."

"How many people are coming?" Meg's eyes sparkled with excitement. "Is it everyone we know, Anna?"

"I think we should keep it small this year," Anna replied. "Just Gino and the girls."

"And Leo," Cassie reminded her. "Bobby will be here by then too, Mom. I say we go all out, invite everyone we know."

"We'll need plenty of food." Sofia rubbed her hands. "I better start making a shopping list."

"Everyone always brings a dish," Anna reminded her. "It's more like a potluck, I guess. Don't go overboard, Mom."

"Nonsense!" Sofia dismissed. "You can never have enough food."

"Don't forget we'll be going to the children's home earlier

that day, Mom. I anticipate spending a few hours there. We won't be back until evening."

Meg perked up when she heard about the children.

"People have started placing gifts under the tree at the café. Did you see that, Anna?"

"Your idea is pure genius, Meg," Cassie praised. "A couple of customers at the bookstore noticed the packages under the tree. I told them how we are collecting them for the kids. They promised to come back with some gifts."

"You're doing a fine thing, sweetie." Sofia kissed the top of Meg's head.

Anna realized Meg herself had been underprivileged for most of her life. She had been moved around from one foster parent to another until a kind couple finally adopted her at the age of sixteen. Anna felt a sense of pride in her granddaughter when she realized Meg hadn't forgotten those less fortunate than her.

"I already told my cookie exchange group to set aside one set of cookies for the kids," she told Meg. "We'll make sure they have plenty of goodies to eat, Meg."

"Can we not talk about food for a moment?" Cassie grumbled goodnaturedly. "Meg wants to share something with us."

"What do you mean, Cassie?" Meg set her plate down.

"Tell us about that guy, Meg." Cassie folded her arms and

raised her eyebrows. "Long brown hair, glasses, leather jacket …"

"Him." Meg sighed. "Just someone I ran into. He came to the café a couple of times."

"Wait a minute." Anna's eyes met Cassie's. "Is this that guy from the college? The one who made you hold up that banner and chant slogans?"

"The same," Meg replied.

"How did I miss him?" Anna was concerned. "Has he been bothering you, Meg? Why haven't you told us about this?"

"Look, it's no big deal." Meg tried to make light of the situation. "He's not important."

"What did he want?" Cassie asked.

"You're talking like fools," Sofia reprimanded them. "What does a young man want from a pretty lady? Bet he was asking her out."

"Is that true?" Cassie looked incredulous. "He looked so unkempt. I hope you said no, Meg."

"I tried to." Meg looked uncomfortable.

"Do you like this young man, child?" Sofia asked kindly.

"I don't know." Meg shrugged. "Phoenix came to the café a couple of times. You were right, Nana. He did ask me out. Wanted to take me to dinner. I turned him down but he kept coming back. So I met him at the Tipsy Whale one evening."

"You should have told me about this, Meg." Cassie sounded hurt. "I would have helped you choose an outfit."

"I wore that new dress Anna bought for me. Then I felt foolish."

"Why?" the three older women chorused.

"It wasn't a date like I thought. He brought a friend with him."

"Ugh!" Cassie looked disgusted. "This guy's not worth your time, Meg."

Anna was more interested in the friend.

"Who did he bring along? Maybe he was fixing you up with this other guy."

Meg laughed.

"Not likely, Anna. Rupert already has a girlfriend. He's dating Alison Gardiner."

"Edward's granddaughter?" Anna burst out. "Now that's a coincidence. What did he talk about?"

Meg frowned.

"He didn't appear sad about Mr. Gardiner's death. In fact, he almost looked happy. Told me he didn't get along with the old man."

"What does this Rupert do?" Sofia grunted. "Must be a layabout."

"Rupert Sadler doesn't believe in working for another man." Meg winced. "Those are his words, not mine. He has a lot of business ideas."

"Let me guess," Anna said grimly. "He asked Edward to sponsor him and the old man declined."

Meg was nodding vigorously.

"The old man wanted him to prove himself. All Rupert had to do was start a business and keep it running for a year."

"Too much for this kid?" Cassie guessed.

"Rupert thinks the young need a head start. It behooves the older generation to give it to them. Especially, filthy rich people like Mr. Gardiner who have millions in the bank."

"This young man is lucky he doesn't live with the Gardiners." Anna shook her head. "He would make a very good suspect with a motive like that."

Meg couldn't hide her excitement.

"But that's just it, Anna. He was right there the night Mr. Gardiner died."

"What?" Anna exclaimed. "Do the police know about this?"

"Why would he tell you that, Meg?" Cassie wondered.

"He was kind of bragging about it." Meg's cheeks turned red. "There's this old apple tree outside Alison's bedroom. Rupert uses it to sneak in many times."

Cassie gave a wolf whistle. Sofia pursed her lips in disapproval.

"I wonder if Gino knows about this." Anna got up and collected their dessert plates.

Meg followed her into the kitchen and started loading the dishwasher.

"I didn't like Rupert."

"What about Phoenix?" Anna hid a smile. "Do you want to go out with him again?"

"He didn't exactly ask me." Meg started scraping a plate. "I don't understand him."

"Are you afraid of what Leo will think about this?"

"Leo is just my friend, Anna."

"If you say so, sweetie. What about this Phoenix guy then? Do you like him?"

Meg blew her cheeks out.

"Phoenix plays basketball with the admissions coordinator at DBU. He offered to get me an interview with him."

"That's good, right?"

"I'm not sure I like Phoenix, Anna. Will it be fair to have him do something for me?"

Meg put the last plate in and shut the dishwasher. Anna motioned her to sit.

"You're thinking too much, Meg. I think this boy is just being nice."

Meg took a deep breath.

"Can people be kind for no reason?"

"Sure they can, dear." Anna patted her hand.

A light drizzle had started that evening. Anna poured freshly brewed coffee into special red stoneware mugs. Cassie had painted reindeer on them when she was ten. Anna couldn't believe those mugs were still intact after so many years.

"Let's go sit by the fire," she said to Meg.

"Can we roast marshmallows?"

"You bet!"

Sofia brandished a list when they entered the living room.

"We are making a huge antipasti platter for your party, Anna. And my special caprese salad with the bocconcini and cherry tomatoes."

"That's great, Mama. How about making your garlic rosemary oil? It will be great with fresh country bread."

"Already thought of that!" Sofia hummed with excitement. "And I'm making my twelve hour balsamic reduction."

Meg and Cassie giggled while Anna patiently heard her mother out.

"We'll help you taste everything, Nana. Right Meg?"

Chapter 13

Anna's arms ached from the heavy bags she carried. Anna and the Firecrackers had spent the morning shopping in the city for presents. They groaned collectively as they walked through the mall's parking lot to Julie's car.

"Don't you remember where you parked?" Anna complained. "You should have noted which section we were in."

The car was finally located and the ladies heaved a sigh of relief.

"Where to?" Julie yawned. "I say we pick up something to eat and head home."

They agreed to grab something from a drive through.

"Do you have to go back to the café?" Mary asked Anna.

"I don't think so. It'll be late afternoon by the time we reach Dolphin Bay. Meg will already have closed up."

"All I want is a hot bath." Julie was weary. "I say we make use of that hot tub of yours, Anna."

"Great idea!" Anna perked up. "That sounds perfect in this weather. I can put a casserole in the oven and then we can just relax in the tub. Dinner will be ready by the time we are done."

"Sofia might beat you to that," Julie laughed. "Just the thought of those hot jets massaging my back makes me feel better already."

They picked up cheeseburgers from their favorite fast food joint along with hand cut fries. Anna and Mary insisted Julie park the car while they ate.

A couple of hours later, they sat in the tub with their eyes closed, breathing in the heady scent of the numerous candles around them. Anna had chosen an assortment of winter scents, combining pine, cinnamon and pumpkin spice.

"Did you get everything on your list?" Mary asked her friends.

"I got something for Cassie, Meg and Mama. And I put in an order for some special jewelry for us."

"What about Gino?" Julie's lip curved into a smile.

"I got him a silk tie."

"When have you seen him wear a tie?" Julie rolled her eyes. "Why not get something monogrammed, like a watch or wallet?"

"Or wine glasses," Mary suggested.

"I don't want to look brazen."

Julie gave her a spiel on how she needed to make the most of the time available to her.

"Any update on the Gardiners?" Mary asked, trying to change the subject.

"I'm pretty much stumped," Anna admitted. "Hard to say anything at this point."

"I'm ready to get out of here." Julie stood up suddenly, examining her wrinkled fingers. "Let's do something useful. I have an idea."

Half an hour later, Anna was dressed and sipping coffee in the living room. Julie had found an old stand in the garage, along with a whiteboard. She had written down three names on it.

"I think we should start with the men. Let's face it. Whoever smothered that poor old man must have had some strength."

"How much strength do you need to hold down a sleeping man?" Mary argued.

"Mary's right." Anna looked at her friends. "But let's go with the men for now."

She looked at the three names Julie had noted on the board.

"Finn O'Malley is the outsider. He is known to be angry. I think he had a grudge against Edward."

"But why wait until this precise moment?" Julie asked. "Hasn't this Finn been living with the Gardiners for a long time?"

"He doesn't actually live in the house," Mary pointed out.

Anna shook her head thoughtfully.

"No. But he could have easily come in through the back door."

"So he did have an opportunity." Julie put a check in front of Finn O' Malley's name.

"Pearson is next." Anna chose the next one. "He's been with the family for decades. And Edward just gave him a raise and settled a pension on him. I think he's loyal to a fault."

"But could he have done it?" Mary asked. "Did he have access to Edward's room?"

Anna thought of the small swinging door connecting the staff wing to the main house. George Pearson had told her there was no lock on that door. So the staff could come and go easily whenever someone rang for them from the main house.

"He did," Anna said reluctantly.

Julie put a check against Pearson's name.

"Rupert Sadler." She read the next name on the board. "I don't know who this is."

"Alison's boyfriend," Anna supplied. "We wouldn't have learned about him if not for Meg."

"He must not be local," Mary observed. "I don't know any Sadlers in Dolphin Bay."

"I never thought of that, Mary." Anna bit her lip. "He asked the old man for money but Edward refused. I'm sure he didn't like that."

"So he had a grudge too." Julie placed a check against Rupert's name. "What about opportunity? Was he anywhere near the mansion on that fateful night?"

"He was!" Anna was triumphant. "Right there in Alison's room. He told Meg himself."

Julie reluctantly added another check against the boy's name.

"I don't know, Anna. If the kid was guilty, he wouldn't advertize the fact that he was in the vicinity of the scene of crime."

"Julie has a point," Mary agreed quietly.

"So this is how it is." Anna waved her hand at the board. "We are stuck until some new information comes along."

Sofia came in holding a platter of cheese and olives with crusty bread. Meg and Cassie followed with bowls of marinated mushrooms and sweet peppers.

"Set that aside, Julie." Sofia sat in her favorite chair. "Time to eat."

Anna didn't sleep well that night. She went over everything she knew about the Gardiners over and over in her mind. Had she missed picking up on some vital clue? What had Sharon told her about her brother?

Anna was already in the kitchen the next morning when her alarm went off. She mixed the batter for her cupcakes, trying to still her mind. She decided to spend an extra ten minutes in the garden. Maybe the fresh air would help soothe her.

An hour later, she suddenly remembered something as she bit into her avocado toast.

"Who was that man with the big sideburns who was flirting with you, Cassie?"

Cassie looked up sleepily from her frosted flakes.

"What?"

"Wake up, Cassie! You remember the Gardiners' holiday party? There was a man there, named after a vegetable, something green."

"Basil?" Cassie laughed. "He called himself a major domo. Or estate manager in plain English."

"Do you have his number?"

"He insisted on giving it to me."

"Use it. Tell him you are meeting him at the Tipsy Whale for lunch."

Cassie rubbed her eyes and tapped some keys on her phone. She told Anna Basil had agreed immediately.

The café kept Anna busy for the next few hours. Julie and

Mary were both busy running errands and had begged off their coffee date. Anna pulled off her apron at 11:30 and went into the bookstore to get Cassie. They walked to the local pub, enjoying the cold sunny day.

Murphy, the pub owner, greeted them cheerfully.

"You're going to love today's special, Cassie."

The Tipsy Whale was famous for its hearty gourmet sandwiches, made with the best quality of produce.

A tanned man with red sideburns waved at Cassie from a booth. He didn't look surprised when Anna joined them.

"Did you find out what happened to the boss, Mrs. Butler?"

Anna guessed the whole town knew what she was up to. Or Basil had been talking to Sharon or Pearson.

"I could use your help."

"Edward Gardiner was the most generous employer anyone could ask for. He didn't deserve to die like that."

"Shall we order first?" Cassie smiled at Basil.

"I recommend the special. You won't find a barbecued chicken sandwich like it anywhere along the coast."

"Not even in Hollywood," Cassie agreed. "That's what I'm getting."

"Who do you think gains from Edward's death?" Anna

asked the major domo. "I know the will hasn't been opened yet. Did he ever mention who was going to inherit everything?"

"Alison," Basil said promptly. "She was the sole heir since Ruth died."

"What about Sharon or Finn O'Malley?"

"I don't think the boss would leave them in the lurch." Basil plunged his straw in his iced tea. "But the bulk of the estate would go to Alison."

Anna sensed there was more coming.

"Why don't you look convinced?"

"That's how it was for the longest time," Basil said thoughtfully. "But there was something afoot. The boss had a lot of meetings with his lawyers."

"Could it have been about some new business deal?" Anna offered.

Basil shook his head confidently.

"There are two sets of lawyers. The boss met with the ones who make his will."

Chapter 14

Cassie drained her glass of fresh squeezed orange juice and laced up her sneakers before stepping out. She slowly made her way to the Coastal Walk. It was cold and windy. The icy wind felt prickly on her skin but Cassie didn't mind. She had been yearning for fresh air and a good long run after indulging in all the rich food her Nana cooked every day.

The Coastal Walk stretched from a small cove at one end to the magnificent Castle Beach Resort at the other. It was the crowning glory of Dolphin Bay. Cassie jogged toward the resort end as usual and collapsed on a strategically placed bench that faced the bay.

She sucked in huge mouthfuls of freezing air, trying to catch her breath. Her eyes watered, her nose ran and she could feel her cheeks burn.

"You're a mess, Cassie."

Teddy Fowler was doing stretches at his usual spot. Cassie had gone to school with him. He and his wife were big fans of Cassie's movies. Cassie often bent Teddy's ear to learn more about what the police thought about a case.

"Do I look that awful?" Cassie pouted. "I'm glad there are no paparazzi hiding in the bushes here."

"You look cute."

"Don't let your wife hear you say that."

"She won't mind," Teddy blushed. "She knows I don't mean it in a bad way."

"How have you been, Teddy?" Cassie pulled a tissue out of her pocket. "Work keeping you busy?"

"I know you're trying to pump me for information about the Gardiner case. You won't get anything out of me."

Teddy's face was set in a smirk.

"Come on! You must have narrowed down a suspect."

Teddy sat down next to Cassie.

"The Gardiners were always a close knit family. They were generous and friendly toward everyone so they have a lot of goodwill in these parts. Can't imagine anyone wanting to harm them."

"So you think one of the family is responsible?"

"That doesn't seem likely either. This one has me stumped, Cassie."

Cassie stood up and started doing jumping jacks, trying to stay warm.

"You're no help."

"I got the invite for your mom's Christmas Eve party. Will you thank her for me?"

They chatted about holiday traditions and gifts. Teddy told her how he was building a model airplane for his boys.

"Bring Meg over for dinner sometime. I'll ask my wife to set it up."

Cassie began a slow, laborious jog back home. After a while, she gave up trying to run and settled into a brisk walk. Sofia stood at the front door with her hands on her hips, clucking with disapproval.

"You must be mad, going out in the cold like that."

"I need to get some exercise in, Nana. A few extra pounds are fine, but I can't look like a pumpkin at my next audition. My agent will have my hide."

"Your mother and Meg have already left for the café."

Cassie pulled off her damp hoodie and walked straight into the shower. Sofia slid a hot omelet onto her plate a few minutes later.

"What are you doing today, Nana?"

Sofia told her she was going to bake some cookies for the cookie exchange.

Cassie headed out, feeling how glad she was Meg was home with them now. Over the years, Cassie had donated a lot of money to different charities for kids, always wondering what her own child was doing for Christmas. In her wildest dreams, she had never believed she would be reunited with her daughter.

A couple of regular customers looked up from their magazines and newspapers when Cassie reached the bookstore. She set about her daily routine, straightening things and dusting the shelves. She was about to walk into the café to talk to Meg when the doorbell jingled. A tall, beautiful woman with emerald eyes and a distinctive dimple came in with a dark haired fella.

"Alison, right?" Cassie greeted the newcomer brightly. "I'm sorry about your grandpa. How are you holding up?"

Alison Gardiner thanked Cassie profusely. She hadn't lost any of her effervescence.

"Old man had to die sometime," the man with Alison chortled. "The timing couldn't be better."

Cassie guessed he was the boy Meg had run into earlier.

"This is my boyfriend Rupert." Alison introduced him. "He's a film director. We were hoping to get some pointers from you."

"I was never involved in the technical side of things," Cassie told them. "Now if there was something you wanted to know about acting, I'm your gal."

"I told you coming here was a waste of time," Rupert hissed at Alison.

"Be quiet, Rupert." Alison smiled endearingly. "Of course we know you're an actress, Cassie. I bet you have plenty of contacts in Hollywood. Maybe you could just introduce Rupert to some studio people you know."

"I can put in some serious money," Rupert preened. "Especially now that old man Gardiner finally croaked."

"How fortunate." Cassie flashed a smile.

"Grandpa was going to finance Rupert," Alison said hastily. "What a pity he's not around."

Cassie promised to make a few calls. Rupert messed around while Alison picked up a couple of the latest bestsellers.

Cassie walked into the café through the connecting arch as soon as Alison left with her outspoken boyfriend.

Anna and the Firecrackers sat at their favorite window table, sipping coffee and eating cookies.

"Try these ginger snaps, Cassie." Mary offered her a heaped plate. "I'm planning to take them to the cookie exchange."

Cassie stuffed a couple of cookies in her mouth before remembering her resolve to cut calories. Then she decided there was ample time to shape up after the holidays. January was boring anyway. Bobby's boot camp would keep her busy.

"Did I hear Alison a few minutes ago?" Anna asked.

Cassie plunged into a vivid description of the merry Alison and her deadbeat boyfriend. The Firecrackers exchanged a knowing look.

"He sounds like a bad one," Mary mumbled.

"My money's on him alright." Julie banged a fist on the

table. "Pearson is too loyal and Finn O'Malley is a decorated veteran. What does this young man have going for him?"

"We can't jump to conclusions." Anna sighed. "The most frustrating thing here is the total lack of evidence."

"Where's Meg?" Cassie asked.

"Out for lunch with that guy from the college," Anna informed her.

"Phoenix?" Cassie's eyebrows shot up. "This should be interesting."

Later that night, the Butler women sat in the living room with Julie and Mary, packing stacks of cookies in transparent wrap, tying them with a red satin ribbon. A fire crackled in the grate, lending some welcome warmth while the wind howled outside.

"Are you going to tell us about your lunch date, Meg?" Cassie couldn't curb her curiosity any longer.

"We just grabbed a sandwich at the Tipsy Whale." Meg tried to look nonchalant. "No big deal."

"Did he bring a friend this time?" Sofia growled.

Meg's cheeks grew pink as she shook her head.

"So it was a proper date then." Anna smiled.

"What did you talk about?" Cassie pressed. "He didn't carry

on about the plight of whales or sea otters or something, did he?"

Meg shook her head.

"We talked about our backgrounds. Phoenix had a hard life growing up."

"So you have something in common," Cassie prompted.

"His mother was a single parent. She worked hard to give him the best of everything. So he wanted to be a lawyer and earn a lot of money, you know. Give his mother all the luxuries she missed while raising him. But then he got into this environment thing. Fighting for the cause means more to him than earning big bucks now. His mother fully supports him."

Sofia pressed her lips together and said nothing.

"Did you tell him about your childhood, dear?" Anna was gentle.

"You don't have to hide anything, Meg," Cassie said seriously. "I'm not going to feel bad if you tell people I dumped you after you were born. It's the truth, however bitter it is."

Anna looked pained.

"Don't be flippant, Cassie. This is why people think you are a cold hearted monster."

"I told him I grew up in the foster system," Meg admitted.

"I hope that didn't turn him off," Anna said.

"He was curious. He asked me a lot of questions."

"So is he doing a bunk or meeting you again?" Julie always liked things cut and dried.

"I think Leo is a nice young man, Meg." Mary offered her opinion softly.

"Phoenix is no match for Leo," Meg agreed shyly. "But I'm not ready to get serious with anyone right now."

"That sounds wise." Anna patted Meg's arm. "At your age, you should just go out and have fun."

"Don't think too much about the future," Cassie added. "You've got us now. We'll steer you right if you fall off the path. Won't we, Mom?"

"We can try." Anna grinned mischievously. "If she's a trailblazer like you, she'll be forging her own way across the world."

"Guys, I'm right here!"

Cassie was surprised to feel her eyes moisten with tears. Was it Dolphin Bay or was it the holiday season that was making her maudlin?

Chapter 15

Anna couldn't stop smiling as she broke eggs into a bowl.

The previous evening had taken an unexpected turn. Meg was busy working with her Seaside Lights committee. She had dragged Cassie along with her. Sofia had finally admitted she was feeling exhausted from all the holiday prep. She was going to take a bowl of minestrone soup to her room and lie in bed the whole evening.

Anna found herself at a loose end after a long time. She was debating between reading Julie's latest romance or watching Downton Abbey reruns when Gino called. He wanted to know if Anna was free for dinner.

A sudden burst of energy propelled Anna to put on a nice frock and dress up. She observed herself in the mirror, wondering if the lines on her forehead had deepened. Feeling reckless, she applied the dark red lipstick Cassie had given her and dabbed some perfume behind her ears.

She was pulling on her winter coat, longing for warmer weather, when Gino arrived. He couldn't stop staring at her.

"You're so beautiful, Anna!" Gino sounded breathless.

Anna felt her pulse thrum against her throat as they drove

to Gino's stately home, set amidst the Mystic Hill vineyard. They stole glances at each other every few seconds but neither of them said anything. Anna felt giddy with excitement and couldn't help the blush that stole over her.

Gino led Anna to his sunken sitting room and lit a few candles. A bottle of wine was breathing on the table and a tray loaded with assorted cheese, olives, fruit and crackers lay beside it. Gino poured the wine and they clinked glasses, toasting each others' health.

"How long has it been since our last date, Anna?"

"It's a wonder we could get away tonight."

"You've been working really hard at the café and it's paying off. People are talking about your cupcakes wherever I go."

Anna asked after Gino's family. His kids had to be overseas that year for work. They were celebrating the holiday abroad along with his grandkids. Gino tried to hide his disappointment.

"You will spend the holiday with us. I won't let you wallow, Gino."

"I'm grateful. I wouldn't dream of being anywhere else."

The talk inevitably turned to the Gardiners.

"I got a call from Edward's estate manager today, Anna. It seems the old guy kept his will in the office safe. Basil had specific instructions regarding when and how to access it."

"Has the will finally been opened?"

Anna told Gino about her meeting with Basil.

"His hunch may be right. The will is missing."

"Are you saying someone stole it?"

Gino shook his head.

"Edward might have been working on creating a new one. He must have discarded the old one. My guess is it had something to do with that big announcement."

"Do you think he was going to disown someone in the family?"

Gino gave a small shrug.

"Hard to say now, Anna. There are some rumors going around, of course. The police think George Pearson knew what was coming. He got nothing in the new will so he bumped the old man off."

"Pearson told us the old man set up a sizeable trust for him."

"What if Edward promised that in a fit of generosity?" Gino wondered. "He could have changed his mind later."

"Do you think the man you knew would do that?"

"Not unless something dire happened." Gino refilled their wine glasses and bit into a cube of cheese.

"Think of this from Pearson's perspective. He's ready to retire and has been promised a nest egg. He has no options other than the largesse of his employer, a reward for 40 years of loyal service. What if that was suddenly taken away?"

"I think I would be blind with fury." Anna was dismayed. "Do you think he killed the old man in a fit of rage?"

"The police believe so," Gino sighed. "Although I think their evidence is circumstantial. Pearson is the only person with motive and opportunity. He wasn't related to Edward and he needed the money."

Anna thought the whole theory was very flimsy.

"Are the police going to arrest Pearson?"

"They plan to bring him in," Gino told her. "Honestly, I feel bad for the poor man."

Anna admitted feeling a bit tipsy. Gino sat up with concern.

"Dinner is ready, Anna. Let's eat."

Although Gino employed a full time cook, he liked to dabble in the kitchen. Anna had experienced his gourmet cooking before and was looking forward to what he was serving that night.

Gino had cooked chicken with sundried tomatoes and spinach. He served it with creamy orzo pasta and a salad.

"This is so good," Anna said between bites. "You're gifted,

Gino. Cooking is more than just following a recipe."

They sat by the fire in the sitting room, enjoying warm apple crumble laced with brandy and bursting with cinnamon.

Neither noticed the time as they talked about every topic on earth while a classic black and white movie played in the background. Finally, Gino reluctantly stood up to drive Anna home.

They held hands on the drive back. Anna blamed the cold for the goose bumps on her arms even though warm air drifted out of the car's vents. They stood before Anna's house and admired the lights. Then it was time to call it a night.

Anna stopped daydreaming when she heard the girls move about in their rooms. She stirred the eggs in the skillet and switched gears, thinking of the unpleasant task that lay ahead.

Cassie and Meg stumbled in, their eyes bright with mischief.

"How was your date, Mom?"

"Why didn't you tell us you were going out, Anna?"

Anna set a platter of scrambled eggs next to olive and cheese muffins and told them to start eating. But she couldn't stop smiling.

The three Butler women headed to the café after breakfast. Anna went into the tiny office she had in the bookstore and placed a call to Craig Rose. She debated meeting him at the café or the diner, then decided on a more secluded place.

Two hours later, Anna was bundled up in her winter coat, hurrying down the Coastal Walk trying to keep warm. A dark bank of clouds hugged the horizon. A fine mist swirled around her, reducing visibility, making everything appear mysterious. Dark figures loomed over her and Anna realized they must be the exhibits the Seaside Lights committee was working on.

Anna slowed as she reached a bench overlooking the bay. It was half a mile from the cafe and she fervently hoped she wouldn't run into anyone she knew.

Craig Rose looked at his watch as Anna approached him. His shock of white hair stood out on the bleak day.

He didn't waste time on any niceties.

"What do you have for me?"

"Your man is in the clear. I have it on good authority that George Pearson will be arrested today."

Craig Rose didn't look convinced.

"Look, I did what you asked. Now tell me about John."

"Not yet. Let the police act. I need to be sure my boy's going to be okay."

"That's not fair!" Anna felt helpless. "We had a deal. You owe me any information you have about my husband."

Craig Rose stood up and started walking away. Anna simmered with anger but there was nothing she could do. She lost track of how long she stood there with her hands in her coat pockets, staring out at the bay. A few droplets fell and a light drizzle started, finally prompting her into action.

"What were you doing out in the cold, Anna?" Meg rushed to take her coat when Anna walked into the café.

Julie and Mary sat at their usual table, drinking coffee.

"Have you lost your mind?" Julie hissed when Anna sat down before them.

Anna felt numb. Would she ever find out who killed her husband? She had been banking on getting some useful information from Craig Rose.

"We know you're hiding something from us," Julie said. "And we know you must have a good reason for it."

"Just promise us you won't do anything rash," Mary said gently. "We are here for you, Anna, no matter what."

"She knows that!" Julie exclaimed. "She has to."

"Thanks." Anna tried to hide her frustration. "There's nothing to tell, girls."

The café was full with holiday shoppers. Anna stayed busy serving the customers while Julie and Mary wrapped presents for the tree. Cassie peeped in from the bookstore and offered to do a sandwich run for lunch.

An hour passed but none of them noticed until Cassie came back in, wild eyed. She dumped a big bag of food on the table and sat down with a thud.

Her cheeks were red from the cold and her chest heaved as she tried to catch her breath.

Anna and Meg walked over, feeling concerned.

"What is it, child?" Julie asked sharply.

"Teddy Fowler came into the Tipsy Whale just as I was leaving." Cassie looked stricken. "George Pearson is dead. The police think he was murdered!"

Chapter 16

Anna wasn't having a good day. The news of George Pearson's death had cast a gloom over her. She didn't understand why. She had barely met the man a couple of times. He hadn't been a friend or even a casual acquaintance. Anna refused to consider what his death meant for her investigation.

Anna couldn't stop the thoughts running wild in her head. Pearson's death had shortened the playing field. The police would look at the remaining people in the Gardiner household as suspects. Finn O'Malley was sure to come under the radar. That wouldn't make Craig Rose happy.

The ornery old man's attitude had rattled Anna. She wondered if he really knew anything about John. Was he just calling her bluff? Until a few weeks ago, Anna had been confident her husband didn't have any secrets from her. She would have bet her life on it. But the news of his infidelity had shocked her to the core. She didn't know what to believe any more.

How long would Craig Rose continue to be difficult? Anna needed to learn everything possible about her husband so she could solve his murder.

Shopping frenzy was at a peak as the holidays approached. Customers streamed in and out of the café at a steady pace. Meg and Anna could barely keep up.

Anna didn't get a chance to relax until she went home later that afternoon. She put her feet up and ate the caponata sandwich Sofia handed her, barely tasting it.

Julie and Mary arrived some time later.

"You look done in, Anna. Are you sure you want to do this now?"

Anna assured Julie she was fine.

They brought out the whiteboard they had worked on a few days ago. Julie took a red marker and put a big cross over George Pearson.

"Rupert Sadler and Finn O'Malley." Julie pursed her lips. "I say O'Malley did it."

"Aren't we forgetting the women?" Mary spoke up. "Alison is strong and healthy. She looks capable of violence."

"What do we know about Alison?" Julie asked. "She's been working at the company for the past few years and was almost ready to take over the reins."

"She wanted Edward to retire," Anna remembered. "In fact, she was hinting at it very openly during the party."

"Did she get along with the old man?" Julie asked. "It's easy to imagine some friction between them. Alison wanted to implement the new and progressive ideas she learned at business school. Edward was old fashioned. Didn't want to stray too far from the tried and tested."

"Do you know this for a fact, Julie?" Anna was amazed. "Or are you just extrapolating."

"Sorry." Julie was shamefaced. "Occupational hazard, you know. I was just trying to get into Alison's character and imagine what she must be feeling."

"You may not be far off," Anna admitted. "But we will need to confirm that."

"Alison was happy at the party, right? Looked like a pampered princess." Julie narrowed her eyes. "But she did keep referring to the big announcement Edward was going to make at Christmas."

"We keep coming back to that," Anna sighed. "I have a feeling it's important."

"I say the old man was grandstanding," Julie dismissed. "He loved to do that."

"We're not getting anywhere with this." Anna yawned.

"I'm going to Paradise Market for more flour and butter." Mary stood up. "Have you decided what cookie you are bringing to the exchange, Anna?"

"I used my tried and tested chocolate chip cookie recipe. Only, I used white chocolate chips and dried cranberries. The girls liked it."

"That sounds festive." Mary nodded.

Julie remembered she was out of milk and decided to go with Mary. Anna went in to rest.

The pungent aroma of garlic sizzling in olive oil woke Anna. She ambled into the kitchen and poured herself a glass of juice. Sofia was stirring a pot of tomato sauce on the stove.

"What are you making, Mama?"

"Tomato basil sauce. You can use it any way you want."

"I was thinking of making chicken parmesan tonight. It's Cassie's favorite meal. And Meg likes it too."

"I suppose you'll be making a pan of tiramisu to go along with it?"

Anna grinned.

"You know me too well."

"I have pictures of Cassie sitting in a high chair, her face smeared with sauce, eating chicken parmesan." Sofia reminisced fondly.

"Can I see them, Nana?" Meg swept in, bringing the scent of the wind and rain along with her. "I've never seen any baby pictures of Cassie."

"They are in my room." Sofia was elated. "Go to the closet and look for a blue shoe box. Bring it out here. We can sit in the living room and go over them."

"Why don't you stay here in the kitchen?" Anna pleaded. "I can look over your shoulder while I cook."

Meg was out in a jiffy, hugging the box close to her chest like it was some long lost treasure. She alternated between sighs and groans and squeals as she went over the old photos. Sofia regaled them with the story behind every picture.

Anna whipped mascarpone cheese for her tiramisu, happy her mother was getting along with Meg.

"How is the Seaside Lights group doing, Meg?" Anna asked. "Is Sally Davis working you too hard?"

"Sally's a dear. She's so patient. You won't believe how forceful the volunteers can be. Like when we were working on deciding a theme for this year. All kind of outlandish suggestions were thrown around. A bunch of guys wanted a Star Wars theme. Another wanted Avengers. Then there was something called Strange Things. I haven't the faintest idea what that is."

"Don't forget Sally's a high school teacher. She's used to dealing with unruly students."

"Which one did you pick?" Sofia asked.

Meg laughed and shook her head from side to side.

"Oh no, Nana. I'm not allowed to talk about it. In fact, Sally warned us about spies."

"Surely that's too much?" Sofia protested.

"Sally said people from the neighboring towns are always on the prowl. They will go to any lengths to find out what we are doing."

"The Seaside Lights trophy is coveted by small towns up and down the coast," Anna told her. "It may not sound like much, but everyone wants to win it."

"Dolphin Bay hasn't won it in the past twenty years," Sofia added. "And it rankles."

The doorbell rang and Meg rushed out to get it. She came back with Gino in tow.

"You're just in time for dinner," Sofia beamed. "Tell your mother it's time to eat, Meg."

"What is Cassie up to?" Anna didn't know when Cassie had come in.

"She was on the phone with Bobby." Meg walked down the hallway and knocked on Cassie's door. "She just got out of the shower."

Anna set out the salad and the bread. She pulled the pan of chicken out of the oven. She noticed Gino seemed distracted.

"More bad news?" Anna held her breath.

"Not exactly." Gino was noncommittal. "Let's do justice to this excellent meal first."

Cassie came out looking excited.

"Is that chicken parmesan I smell? Thanks Mom!"

"It's my way of thanking you for taking care of the

bookstore, Cass. I really appreciate it."

Dinner was lively. Sofia regaled them with the shenanigans of her cronies at the senior community. They voted to eat dessert in the living room.

Gino set his plate aside a few minutes later and refused a second helping.

"The police chief called me earlier today, Anna," he said gravely. "You remember they had found a residue in Edward's nostrils?"

"You did say something about it, Gino."

"Well, they traced it to the type of bag it must have come from. They are positive they will find it somewhere on the Gardiner estate."

"How will that help them narrow down a suspect?" Anna looked skeptical.

"They didn't share that with me. But it's obvious who they are going after, now that Pearson is no longer in the picture."

"You don't mean Finn O'Malley?" Anna hoped she didn't sound as desperate as she felt. "That's ridiculous."

"He lives on the estate, Anna. Word around town is he had a grudge against the old man. Didn't you say he had open access to the main house?"

"Finn is a decorated war veteran." Anna was blushing furiously. "He deserves some respect, Gino. I thought you would understand that, having served yourself."

"I'm not saying …"

"Don't forget he was injured." Anna cut him off. "Someone said he has an artificial limb."

"A bionic leg," Gino said gently. "I know that, Anna. But he has plenty of upper body strength. And I know Finn. He's an honorable man but he's irascible."

"You'll say he has mental issues next." Anna felt her cheeks grow warm.

"Relax, Anna. I'm not saying anything. Please be reasonable."

Meg and Sofia were looking stunned. Cassie was the only one who dared to tackle Anna.

"Why are you all riled up, Mom? You barely know Finn O'Malley."

Chapter 17

Anna tried to focus on frosting her cranberry sage cupcakes the next morning. She cringed when she thought of her behavior the previous night. Gino hadn't stayed long.

Sofia had told her she was a fool and stomped off to bed. Meg and Cassie didn't say anything, choosing to watch one of Cassie's old movies. Anna had made some chamomile tea and changed into her softest old pajamas before climbing into bed. She realized Craig Rose had her all twisted. Anna read for a while and came up with a game plan. Sleep had come easily after that.

"Good Morning, Anna." Meg looked cherubic as she came into the kitchen, dressed in a red turtleneck.

"Can you do without me for a while today, Meg? Mary will help you."

"Sure. Are you going on a secret shopping trip?" Meg winked. "I don't need anything else, Anna."

"You promised I could buy as many gifts as I wanted, Meg. I'm your grandmother and it's my job to spoil you."

"But …"

"Don't worry. I have a different mission today. Julie and I are going to the Gardiner estate."

Cassie came in and poured her favorite sugary cereal in a bowl. Sofia was right behind her and started peeling a boiled egg. A steady hum of conversation filled the kitchen.

Anna sprinkled hot sauce on her avocado toast and tuned them out, trying to marshal her thoughts. She hoped Finn O'Malley would be willing to answer her questions.

Julie called and promised to meet Anna at the café around ten. Black clouds threatened to burst open any time as Meg and Anna loaded the van and drove to the café. A bunch of people were already waiting for them on the sidewalk.

Anna barely got a chance to look up during the early morning rush. Meg nudged her and pointed to the grandmother clock that stood at the entrance.

"Julie will be here any minute, Anna."

Anna hastily packed four assorted cupcakes in a box and fixed her lipstick. She was peering through the glass windows when Julie pulled up outside.

"Are we going to the main house first, Anna?"

"I didn't think that far ahead."

Julie gave her an exasperated look. They seemed to have come to a silent decision by the time they reached the mansion.

They knocked on the door of the main house and waited. Anna almost expected Pearson to open the door and greet them with a bow.

"Looks like nobody's home, Julie."

"Or they are not used to getting the door when someone knocks. Why don't we try to find this cottage ourselves?"

Anna pulled her coat closer and nodded. She looked around and spotted two meandering paths disappearing into the woods.

"Let's try this first."

She started walking down the one on the right. Julie followed her, grumbling about the cold.

Anna turned around a bend and almost walked into a wall. A tall, rugged man wearing camo pants and a white t-shirt looked down at her. His blue eyes were deep as the bay. Anna wondered what secrets they hid.

A dog barked and Anna stooped down to pet the black and tan German Shepherd watching her intently with his tongue hanging out.

"Say hello to the ladies, Chief," the man ordered.

The dog immediately sat down and held out a paw. Anna smiled and shook it.

"Anna, this is Finn O'Malley." Julie offered an introduction.

The man tipped his head slightly, acknowledging Anna.

"I was hoping to talk to you, Finn. It's important."

Finn turned around wordlessly and started walking down the path. Anna and Julie followed him. Two minutes later, they reached a small dwelling in a clearing, surrounded by towering pines.

"This is my cottage," Finn told them, scratching his blonde stubble. "We can go in here."

"Sounds good." Anna nodded and walked directly into a small sitting room.

A shabby couch covered in pet hair faced a giant flat screen TV. The two armchairs placed around the sofa didn't look any cleaner.

Anna picked a chair and gingerly sat on the edge. She told Finn about her background in solving murders.

"So you're like an amateur detective. My Ruth loved reading those books about the red haired girl who liked to solve crimes. Aren't you a bit older than that?"

"Nancy Drew was fictional," Julie smirked. "Anna here is the real deal. Many people in Dolphin Bay will vouch for her."

Finn stood with his hands folded, his feet planted apart, a frown marring his brow. Anna hoped he would sit down. She had a crick in her neck staring up at him.

"What does this have to do with me?"

Chief left his master's side and leapt up on the couch. He stared dolefully at Anna, waiting for an answer.

"I promised someone I would look into Edward Gardiner's death. And now, Pearson's too, I guess."

"And you suspect me of killing the old man?" Finn looked unfazed.

"I'm talking to everyone who had access to Edward."

"But you must think I have a motive."

He finally sat down and began stroking his dog. Chief licked Finn's hand and rested his head on his lap.

"Word around town is that you didn't get along with Edward. They say you blamed him for your wife's death."

Finn's mouth hardened.

"Ruth's death was a fluke. It would be wrong to blame anyone for it."

Anna saw him curl his fists and bury them deep in the couch. Chief whimpered.

"I'm sorry, I didn't mean to bring up any painful memories."

"I should've been there. I will never forgive myself for that."

Anna sensed the raw pain in Finn's voice. She could empathize with him.

"You must have thought of her every time you looked at Edward."

"That's why I live here," Finn told her. "Ruth was the spitting image of the old man, from the emerald eyes to the cute dimple. The Gardiners are the only connection I have to my Ruth. Being here made me feel close to her."

"You didn't nurse a secret grudge?" Julie needled. "How do we know you weren't waiting for the right opportunity to get revenge?"

"Edward was family. I liked hanging out with him."

Finn stood up and began pacing the room.

"What about the others? Have you considered Sharon? I say she's been wronged all her life. Her father was kinda old fashioned so he left the entire estate to Edward. She just got an allowance."

"Must be a big one," Anna observed. "She isn't exactly hurting for money."

"Sharon had access to millions," Finn admitted and snapped his fingers. "But Edward could take it away like that."

"I wouldn't be comfortable living that way." Julie agreed. "But she must have been used to it."

"Did something happen recently?" Anna asked Finn. "Something that might have threatened Sharon's position?"

"The old man hinted at it. He was going to make a big announcement."

Anna's pulse quickened.

"What was it about? Did he give any clues?"

"Edward was very happy about it, but very secretive. He talked about how his announcement was going to change things around here."

"Did that make you nervous?"

"I lived here and ate his food, lady. But I was used to living on less. And I have my pension to fall back on."

"What about the others?"

Finn hesitated.

"They don't exactly confide in me. But the anxiety levels in the main house were high. Then the lawyers started coming in. I think they all thought the old man was changing his will."

"Was he?" Julie sat forward expectantly.

"Sharon asked the old man about it, just before the holiday party. He laughed and told her to be patient. Everything would be revealed on Christmas morning."

"What else?" Anna sensed Finn was holding back.

"He said they were going to get the biggest shock of their lives."

Anna thought the old man had tempted fate. He had created uncertainty in the minds of his family, instigating one of them to take action.

"Martha, the maid, told us you had a big fight with Edward." Anna waited for Finn to respond.

"I don't remember any such thing." Finn glowered at them.

Anna remembered what Gino had told her about Finn's temperament. She sensed he was about to erupt.

"Thank you for talking to us, Finn." Anna stood up. "And thank you for your service."

She belatedly remembered the cupcakes she had brought and handed over the box to him.

"Please let me know if you think of anything else."

"Am I going to be arrested?" Finn asked point blank.

"You have nothing to worry about if you are innocent." Anna hoped she sounded confident. "I'm going to find out what happened."

A light rain was falling when they stepped out of the cottage. Anna and Julie huddled in their jackets and walked briskly down the path.

"Did you see his bulging biceps?" Julie asked as she climbed into her big SUV and turned the heat on full blast.

Anna waved her hands over the vent, impatiently waiting for the air to grow warm.

"Were you checking him out, Julie?" Anna's mouth dropped open. "Are you going to be one of those panthers now?"

"You mean cougar," Julie corrected her. "Of course I wasn't looking at him like that, Anna. I was thinking how easy it would be for him to hold an old man down and suffocate him."

Chapter 18

Anna stared at the almost empty display case in the café. A couple of muffins and two sugar cookies were all they had left.

"Are you sure we don't have more?" she asked Meg.

"Blame it on the weather." Meg laughed heartily.

The sun had decided to shine brightly that day, bringing the tourists in droves.

"Looks like the entire state of California want to do their holiday shopping today," Anna sighed. "We're going to run out of everything before 11."

"We can take the rest of the day off and do something," Meg suggested.

"Like what?" Anna muttered. "Mama's wrapping our presents today, remember? So we can't go home."

Cassie breezed in from the bookstore.

"We sold more books today than on Black Friday. We should celebrate."

"Great idea, Cassie!" Anna beamed at the girls. "We are going out for lunch."

"To the Yellow Tulip?" Meg brightened. "They have a chili and corn bread special today."

"We can do better than that." Anna took Meg by the shoulders and whirled her around. "You'll see."

"What's the plan, Mom?" Cassie looked amused.

"It's a beautiful sunny day in December and I'm taking my girls out for lunch. That's all you need to know for now."

Anna flipped the café sign to 'Closed' half an hour later. She called out to Cassie and Meg and freshened her lipstick. The deep red shade was beginning to grow on her.

Cassie brought her ancient Mercedes convertible around. Meg climbed into the back seat while Anna shook her head in disbelief.

"Aren't you going to put the top up?"

"It's broken, Mom," Cassie giggled. "We can still walk to the Yellow Tulip."

Anna muttered under her breath and got in.

"We are going to the Castle Beach Resort. I hear their new chef does an excellent lunch."

Cassie drove to the luxury resort, grumbling about how far it was by road. The route was scenic and they enjoyed the vistas of the towering pines and the rocky cliffs. The bay stretched as far as the eye could see, shimmering in the golden sunlight.

The concierge welcomed Anna and the girls warmly. He explained that Charlie Robinson, the genial owner, was out of town on business. They were escorted to a table that overlooked the water, giving them a grand view of the area.

Anna chose the chef's tasting menu for all of them and accepted a sparkling drink from the server. It had muddled cranberries, giving it a festive look.

"How was your date last night, Meg?" Cassie asked.

"I forgot all about it!" Anna exclaimed. "Did that Phoenix behave himself?"

"We barely got a chance to talk." Meg pursed her mouth. "I had no idea we were going to meet Alison and Rupert."

"So it was a double date?" Cassie shrugged. "It does have some advantages. You have someone to talk to if things get awkward. And there's safety in numbers. Remember that, Meg."

"Phoenix said it was a coincidence." Meg didn't look convinced. "Anyway, that Rupert was talking so much I could barely get a word in. I don't like that guy."

The server brought some appetizers. There were shot glasses of lobster bisque. Savory crab puffs and fried ravioli sprinkled with fresh parmesan vied for attention.

Anna popped a crab puff in her mouth and narrowed her eyes.

"What did he say this time?"

"He was bragging about the time he got arrested for assault and battery."

Anna and Cassie sat up with a jerk.

"What?" Cassie croaked. "Who did he beat up?"

"His grandpa." Meg drained a glass of bisque and speared a ravioli with her fork. "They argued over something and the grandpa held back his allowance. Rupert punched him in the face and stormed out. He broke the poor man's nose, Anna. A neighbor heard him crying for help and called the police."

"He's a nasty piece of work." Cassie was alarmed. "Stay away from him, Meg."

"I didn't go looking for him." Meg twisted her mouth. "I don't know why Phoenix hangs out with him. They are complete opposites."

"This Phoenix doesn't look very discerning," Anna frowned. "I'm not sure I approve of him, Meg."

"Are you for real, Mom?" Cassie burst out. "This isn't the dark ages. Meg doesn't need your permission to date someone."

Meg looked uncomfortable. She stared at the ground while they were served tiny lamb meatballs with a creamy yogurt and mint dip along with a citrus fruit salad.

"I don't mind, Cassie," Meg spoke up. "I like that Anna is looking out for me."

"You're smart enough to make your own choices, Meg." Anna placed a hand on Meg's shoulder. "I didn't mean to be high handed. But I'm not sure if you like this young man."

"Neither am I," Meg smiled.

They sighed in unison as the main course was brought out, individual pot pies with buttery crusts with a side of the truffle mac and cheese Anna loved.

"Did you talk to Alison?" Cassie asked Meg. "How is she coping?"

"She seems to be doing great. Asked if I wanted to go shopping with her."

"Sounds just like Sharon." Anna dug her fork into the pot pie. "These Gardiners have a weird way of handling grief."

"Did you meet Sharon again?" Cassie asked her.

"Not since I spoke to Finn," Anna replied. "She was in the city yesterday, shopping for presents."

"What about Mr. Samuels?" Cassie asked. "I wonder why the Chronicle hasn't printed any article on the Gardiners yet. I would have expected some human interest piece by this time."

"You're right." Anna took a bite of the rich and creamy pot pie and moaned with pleasure. "Have you tasted this, Cassie? It's pure heaven!"

Cassie obliged and took a bite.

"This is really good, Mom. We must compliment the chef." She tasted the mac and cheese and licked the spoon. "Doesn't Mr. Samuels come to the café a lot?"

"He does," Anna nodded. "He asks me if I have any new leads every morning. I ask him the same. He said I can go over to the Chronicle offices any time to check his notes."

"Not a bad idea, Mom. Why don't you deputize Meg?"

Meg had been busy inhaling the food. She could barely keep her eyes open.

"Where are you sending me, Cassie?"

"Can you go to the Dolphin Bay Chronicle and do some research for me?" Anna asked.

"Will Mr. Samuels be there too?" Meg asked. "He makes me feel so dumb."

"That's the high school teacher in him," Cassie laughed. "I felt like that too when I was in his class."

"Ian Samuels is harmless," Anna assured Meg. "And he's a kind man. He would never belittle anyone, least of all, a student."

"I guess it's all in my head," Meg admitted. "What am I looking for, Anna?"

Anna paused as the army of servers arrived with their dessert. The three Butler women couldn't hide their amazement at the exquisitely plated dish.

"This is like, five or six desserts in one," Meg exclaimed. "It's a piece of art."

Cassie was more used to gourmet dining. She whacked the dome of chocolate before her and cried with delight at the smaller dome inside. A tap on it caused molten chocolate to flow from all sides on to a scoop of gelato.

None of them spoke until they had scraped their plates clean and licked their spoons dry.

"Tell her what she's doing at the Chronicle, Mom." Cassie patted her stomach and groaned.

"What do we know about the Gardiners?" Anna asked. "Nothing other than Gino's version and the little that the staff or Finn O'Malley told us. Sharon or Alison have been practically useless in this aspect."

"Don't forget the gossip around town," Cassie reminded her.

"That's right!" Anna beamed. "Gossip. Or news. And what's the most authentic source of news in town?"

"The Chronicle archives!" Cassie exclaimed. "Brilliant, Mom."

Anna bobbed her head eagerly.

"Go to the Chronicle and read up on the Gardiners, Meg. Go back a hundred years if you have to. But find out everything that was written about them. Who knows? It might give us some insight into the family."

Meg looked uncertain.

"What if I don't find anything?"

"That's impossible. The Chronicle will have accounts of births and deaths at the very least. The Gardiners have been philanthropists for three generations. There must be several articles written about them."

Meg finally began to look interested.

They lingered over their coffee, digesting the heavy meal, enjoying the view. Half an hour later, Cassie dropped Meg off outside the Chronicle. Anna was spending the rest of the day at Bayside Books, going over the accounts.

The sun was just setting over the horizon when Cassie pulled up outside the Chronicle that evening. Meg was waiting for them, bouncing on her toes, clutching a paper in her hands.

"What did you find?" Anna asked urgently, picking up on Meg's excitement.

"There were dozens of old articles on the Gardiners." Meg flung the paper in Anna's lap and jumped into the back seat. "This one seemed most interesting."

Anna stared at the grainy black and white picture. It showed a young couple huddled together in a booth at some restaurant.

"Is that Sharon?" she muttered after closer inspection. "Who's that with her?"

Her eyes grew wide as she read the caption beneath the photo.

Heiress caught snuggling with the butler.

What was Sharon doing, having dinner with Pearson in a restaurant?

Cassie snatched the paper from Anna's hands and stared at it.

"Wow Meg! You got the money shot!"

Chapter 19

Anna sat in her living room with Julie and Mary. Sofia had invited them for dinner. Luckily, Julie had just finished a section of her book and needed a break. Mary's husband had his weekly poker game. So they had both eagerly accepted.

Sofia had cooked up a storm. There was fresh made pasta to go with baked fish for dinner. The antipasti tray was set out next to the wine. As if all this wasn't enough, Sofia was making three kinds of bruschetta as an appetizer.

"You know the Gardiners well, Julie," Anna said. "Do you remember anything about Sharon and George Pearson?"

Julie took a sip of her wine and nodded approvingly.

"That picture you have must be thirty years old, Anna. I was a bumbling twenty something at that time. The Gardiners were definitely not aware of my existence then."

"I thought you were friends with Sharon." Anna nibbled on a piece of smoked gouda, her favorite.

Julie shook her head.

"She was a secretary or something for some women's group in the area. They invited me as keynote speaker. That's when I met her. Must have been around five or six years ago."

"You were a famous author by that time," Mary nodded.

"Sharon and I got along somehow," Julie continued. "Although I don't know why. We have nothing in common. She invited me to a couple of soirees at the family mansion. Then I met the old man."

"What about you, Mary?" Anna asked hopefully. "Didn't you say your daughter was friends with Ruth?"

"Ruth often came to our house. The girls had play dates when they were kids. Then they had slumber parties. She stayed over a lot even when they were in high school."

"You must have met Sharon?" Anna probed. "Who coordinated all these visits? Or dropped the girls off at school?"

"Ruth and Alison had a nanny. And they had a personal car and driver to take them where they wanted. I don't think Sharon was involved in their day to day activities. Anyway, she never came over or introduced herself."

Sofia came out to check on them.

"Which one do you like more?" she asked, pointing toward the bruschetta. "Roasted mushroom and rosemary or sundried tomato and goat cheese?"

Julie hastily picked one up and took a bite.

"Everything you cook is good, Sofia."

"How close was Sharon to George Pearson?" Anna mused.

"Was this photo just a coincidence or was it a casual date?"

"You think she was being rebellious?" Mary asked.

"She looks quite old in this picture," Julie noted, peering at the piece of paper again. "I'd say mid twenties or late twenties."

"I'm going to ask Meg to continue her research at the Chronicle," Anna told them. "If we're lucky, there might be more articles about them."

"What about going to the horse's mouth?" Mary asked. "Why not ask Sharon herself?"

"I doubt she will admit it." Anna spread some herbed cheese on a cracker. "Especially if it was hush hush."

"Who's she hiding from now?" Julie smirked. "Edward is gone. So is George Pearson. Sharon is the oldest in the family now."

"Why do you think an old affair matters now, Anna?" Mary asked quietly.

"Don't you see?" Anna cried. "A man in love will do anything for his woman."

"Even kill for her?" Julie was skeptical. "What are you getting at, Anna?"

"What if Sharon and Pearson were in collusion?" Anna's eyes were wide as she explained her theory. "Sharon was afraid she would get nothing in the new will. So she talked Pearson into killing the old man."

"George Pearson was considerably shorter than Edward," Julie mused. "But he would still tower over a sleeping person."

"Sharon could have been there with him." Anna's face was animated.

"Go on," Julie said, picking up some cured meat. "Let's play out this fantasy."

"It's completely plausible, Julie." Anna reddened. "Sharon convinced poor George Pearson to do away with her brother. Then she got him out of the way herself."

"So Sharon is a cold blooded woman responsible for not one but two murders?" Julie didn't look convinced.

"Why don't I talk to the women in my knitting club?" Mary asked gently. "If there were any rumors about Sharon dating her butler, they are sure to remember."

Julie waved at the board with the names on it.

"Does that mean you don't suspect O'Malley or that kid, Anna?"

"I don't think we can rule them out yet." Anna frowned. "Wonder why Alison is dating that Rupert. Edward couldn't have approved of him."

Meg came out, looking freshly showered. She had been on the phone with her adoptive parents.

"Mom and Dad have a big surprise for me," she beamed. "I

hope it's a car."

"How are you going to get it here?" Anna asked, trying not to picture Meg driving cross country through icy roads and blizzards.

"We talked about it." Cassie breezed in and sat down next to Julie. She popped an olive in her mouth. "I will fly there and Meg and I will drive back to Dolphin Bay from Iowa. It will be a nice road trip."

"Isn't it early to make plans for summer?" Anna avoided looking at the girls.

"Summer! We are talking about January, Mom."

Julie sensed what was coming and hastily changed the subject.

"Do you think Alison is serious about her boyfriend?" she asked Meg.

"They barely talk to each other." Meg rolled a piece of meat, cheese and apricot together and popped it into her mouth. "Don't see why Alison hangs out with him."

"Can you try to get it out of her?" Anna was hopeful. "Why don't you girls meet for coffee or something? She sounds like a good friend to have."

"Alison is a spoiled brat, Mom." Cassie looked worried. "I'm not sure she's a good influence."

Meg laughed.

"No offense, Cassie. But I've been around the block a few times. I can take care of myself."

Anna tried not to think of the hardships Meg might have undergone in the various foster homes she had lived in.

Sofia hollered from the kitchen, announcing it was time to eat.

"The woman from the children's home called." Anna felt subdued as she twirled pasta on her fork.

"Did you tell them about all the gifts people are leaving at the café and the bookstore?" Cassie asked eagerly. "The kids are going to be happy on Christmas morning."

"She was very grateful," Anna nodded. "But she did have a request."

Everyone looked up at Anna.

"People donate towels and blankets, even winter coats and socks, so they have plenty of those in stock. But the kids could use personal hygiene items like tooth brushes and razors."

"Deodorant, too, Anna," Meg supplied.

"We haven't bought any gifts for the kids yet," Julie spoke up. "Why don't we pool our money and go buy this in bulk?"

"Great idea, Julie!" Sofia clapped her hands. "I'm going to write you a check soon as we finish eating."

Julie and Mary went home after dessert. Sofia declared she wanted an early night. The Butler women played some board games for a while until Cassie started yawning. That set everyone off. Anna collapsed on her bed and fell into a deep sleep.

Dark skies greeted Anna the next morning. But nothing could dampen her spirits. She was meeting Gino for breakfast at the Yellow Tulip.

She finished baking and dressed quickly, glad she could depend on Meg to open the café. She walked to the diner, enjoying the crisp air fragrant with the scent of pine and roasted chestnuts.

Gino sat in a booth at the back, reading the Chronicle. He greeted Anna with a hug and made sure she was comfortable.

The waitress came and poured coffee, giving them both a knowing look. Gino ordered an egg white omelet with grilled vegetables and wheat toast. Anna opted for the same.

"No biscuits and gravy today?" she teased, adding cream to her coffee.

Gino tore open a packet of raw sugar and handed it to her.

"I ran into Teddy Fowler yesterday. He told me the police had spent the day searching the Gardiner property. They found something."

Anna set her coffee mug down and braced herself for bad news.

"There's a storage shed attached to Finn O'Malley's cottage. It contained a box of plastic bags."

"And the police think one of these bags was used to kill Edward?"

"They are running some forensics on the bags now."

Anna placed her hands around the coffee mug, trying to warm them.

"This doesn't look good for Finn O'Malley."

Chapter 20

Anna felt dismayed as she stared at the slender man before her. She thought he was being unkind.

"You don't have an ounce of Christmas spirit," she said bitterly. "Why do you bother to dress for the holidays?"

Craig Rose looked seraphic, wearing a red and green cardigan with Santa Claus and his sleigh embroidered on it.

"We had a deal, Mrs. Butler. You haven't done your part yet. The police are going to arrest my boy any minute now."

"I was very clear," Anna said sharply. "I will not be protecting a guilty person."

"But he isn't!" Craig Rose was petulant. "Finn is as innocent as a newborn babe. He's just being framed."

"Things don't look good for him," Anna warned. "Forensic evidence does not lie."

"But it can be planted," Craig Rose insisted. "What kind of detective are you anyway? Not a very good one, I'd say."

"I'm not a trained detective," Anna protested. "All I can do is ask questions and process the information I have."

"If anything happens to Finn, the deal's off."

"That's not fair!" Anna cried. "I have done everything you asked. You need to cough up now. Tell me what you know about John."

Craig Rose stood up and shook his head.

"Finn O'Malley saved lives. Dozens of them. Do you honestly think he would strangle an old man in his sleep?"

Anna watched the old man walk away yet another time. He got her hot and bothered every time. Anna forced herself to calm down and change her perspective. What would she have done if Craig Rose had not been in the picture?

She walked over to the counter in a daze and began serving the customers, barely noticing a young man who kept going to the back of the line.

"What is he up to?" Meg muttered to herself.

Anna's head snapped up and she finally looked around.

"Is something wrong, Meg?"

"Phoenix is here and he's acting weird." Meg frowned. "I don't know why he keeps coming here, Anna."

"Why don't you ask him to dinner tonight?" Anna said gently. "We can all meet him properly then."

Sally Davis arrived with a contingent of women, Mary among them. Anna had completely forgotten the cookie exchange ladies were meeting that morning. Sally and her cronies joined a bunch of tables together and settled down.

Anna pulled the plastic wrap off a big tray of cupcakes and took it over to the women. Meg followed with the coffee.

Sally waved a paper in the air.

"Just one week for the cookie exchange, ladies. You need to finalize your entries today."

"Are we doing it at the gazebo like every year?" Anna asked.

"Weather permitting," Sally nodded. "If it rains, we thought we would have it here, Anna."

"That's fine by me." Anna was pleased. "The café will be free at 4 PM."

Sally started reading her list.

"Chocolate chip, oatmeal raisin, cranberry white chocolate, snicker doodle, ginger snaps, pumpkin spice, thumbprint, shortbread, pecan …"

Anna reminded the ladies to bring an extra dozen cookies each for the children's home. The gathering broke up shortly. Anna pulled Mary aside and waved goodbye to the others.

"Is Julie here yet?" Mary asked. "I'm driving down to San Jose after we eat."

The Firecrackers were going to the China Garden restaurant for their weekly lunch.

"She's meeting us there," Anna told her. "Just let me put

on my coat, Mary."

They walked down Main Street to the restaurant, admiring all the pretty shop fronts. Julie had already ordered for them.

Anna added some chili sauce to her orange chicken and took a bite. She loved the combination of the hot, sweet and tangy flavors.

Julie asked what was going on with the Gardiners. Anna brought them up to speed with what Gino had told her.

"Any luck digging up Sharon's past?" she asked Julie.

"I talked to a couple of women I know about Sharon," she told them. "She's always been single as far as they remember."

"We know her marital status, Julie. What about any flings?"

"None of them mentioned anything like that."

"So she's either been very discreet or the photo meant nothing." Anna sighed.

"Why don't we go talk to Finn?" Julie asked. "I feel I need to burn off all this rice."

"Count me out," Mary said, breaking open her fortune cookie. "I'm driving to San Jose now. I'm on babysitting duty tonight."

Julie drove them to the Gardiner estate. The day had turned

gloomier while they were at lunch. Lightning streaked across the sky and thunder roared over the horizon. Anna tried to ignore the sinister thoughts clouding her head.

They walked down the path to Finn's cottage after Julie had parked her car. He stood outside, playing with Chief.

"I'm waiting for the police," he told them. "They are going to take me away."

Anna felt sorry for him.

"Don't give up hope yet, Finn."

Chief came and nudged her. Anna took the ball from his mouth and flung it wide. The dog bounded after it happily.

"Can you tell us about the bags?" Anna asked Finn. "How many people know where you keep them?"

"Everyone knows." Finn shrugged. "They are poop bags. For Chief, you know. I order them in bulk."

"Don't you lock that shed?" Julie asked.

Finn looked surprised.

"I don't even lock my front door, lady. There's no need to. This is private property."

"What about the bags?" Anna reminded him gently.

"You see how friendly Chief is. People take him on walks all the time. They like talking to him, I guess."

"They take a poop bag with them every time?" Julie narrowed her eyes.

Finn showed them the leash he was holding. A plastic bag hung from it.

"That's the rule. You never know when the dog will dump."

"I'm sorry. Who took him for walks?" Anna asked.

"All of them." Finn scratched a spot near his eye. "Aunt Sharon, Alison, Pearson, the cook, the maid ... even Edward."

"Do they ask you before they take the dog out?" Julie pressed.

"Of course not!" Finn gave them a queer look.

"Think back to a couple of days before the old man died," Anna said. "Can you recollect who took Chief out then?"

"I couldn't tell you that." Finn looked worried. "I don't remember."

"This might be important, Finn." Anna patted his arm. "Why don't you give it some thought?"

Finn turned around and started walking away. He whistled slowly to summon the dog. Chief ran after him.

"Nice!" Julie grimaced. "That's what you get for helping out."

Anna felt sorry for the young man.

"I think we might have pushed too far. Finn was hurt badly in the war. We don't know the extent of his injuries."

They started walking back to the car.

"What about going to the main house?" Julie asked. "Sharon might be in."

"I don't want to show my hand yet," Anna said. "Let's just go home."

Alison came out of the main house just then. She greeted them with a wave and started walking toward them.

"Are you here to meet my aunt?"

Anna didn't know what to say.

"Done with your Christmas shopping?" Julie asked brightly.

Alison gave them a knowing look.

"Why are you trying to distract me?"

Her eyes narrowed in comprehension.

"Did you just meet that scoundrel Finn? Haven't the police taken him away yet?"

"You don't like Finn, huh." Anna watched Alison closely.

"Don't be fooled by his medals," Alison fumed. "He's diabolical. Has an eye on my fortune. He's been plotting to take control of my money ever since he got here."

"What makes you say that?" Anna asked.

"He had it all planned. He got on Grandpa's good side first. Then he started coming to work. He acted like Grandpa was going to hand him the reins of the company."

"I thought you were Edward's successor, Alison." Julie stroked the girl's ego. "Isn't that what you were saying at the holiday party?"

"I've been working at the company for five years. I worked in every department, trying to understand the finer aspects of running the business. Grandpa was grooming me to take over one day. He had promised!"

"What about Ruth?" Anna asked. "Didn't she get an equal share?"

"Ruth was always a homebody. She was happy playing house with her husband."

"But she's gone now," Anna reminded her. "You are the only heir, I guess."

"That's what I thought," Alison said bitterly. "Then Grandpa started dropping all those hints. He was going to make a big announcement."

"You thought it had something to do with Finn?"

"I did at first," Alison nodded. "But I must have been wrong."

"You are not making any sense," Julie grumbled.

"Don't you see? Finn must have found out what Grandpa's announcement was. That's why he killed him."

Chapter 21

Anna waited impatiently for Gino to arrive. Mary and Julie had come in after lunch. The café had closed an hour ago. Cassie was next door at Bayside Books. She kept peeping in between ringing purchases.

"What's taking him so long?" Julie tapped her fingers on the table. "Didn't you say they started at 10 AM?"

"They were supposed to." Anna expelled a breath. "Gino's phone is switched off so there's no way to know what's going on there."

"Why don't we go for a walk?" Mary suggested. "I could use some fresh air."

"Better than just sitting around, I guess," Julie grumbled.

They stood up and got their coats, ready to step out. The door opened, bringing in a blast of cold air along with Gino.

"Sorry to keep you waiting, Anna."

"It's okay, Gino. Just tell me who gets it all."

An unexpected development had taken place two days ago. Edward Gardiner's manager Basil had continued searching for the missing will. He had found it stuck in a file containing some old contracts. The lawyers had confirmed that it was genuine.

There was a lot of speculation regarding where the will was found. Had Edward been in the process of making a new one? Had he taken the will out of the safe, meaning to destroy it? How had it ended up in the old file?

The general consensus had been that Edward Gardiner misplaced the will by accident. The lawyers wouldn't reveal why they had been meeting the old man before his demise.

Sharon scheduled a reading at the mansion. Gino had been invited since he was a beneficiary.

"Don't you want to know what the old man left me?" Gino teased.

"Some souvenir, no doubt," Anna dismissed. "I just hope it's not a ghastly hunting trophy."

"It's not." Gino grew sober. "It's a chess set. The same one we used to play with."

"Is it expensive?" Julie asked.

"It's made of the finest wood and every piece is carved by hand. My guess is it costs about ten thousand dollars."

"Wow!" the women exclaimed.

"Doesn't matter," Gino shrugged. "As far as I'm concerned, it's priceless. I'm never going to sell it."

"He left you the right thing," Anna murmured.

"Edward prided himself on being fair to people. He kept his promise to Pearson."

Gino explained how Edward had set up a pension fund for the old retainer. He had also bought a small house in town for him. Sadly, Pearson would never know how much his employer had valued him.

"What about Sharon?" Julie rushed ahead. "Did she get half of everything?"

"She gets half the family jewels." Gino scratched his chin thoughtfully. "She has a very generous income for life. Think six figures a month. And she has a stake in the mansion as long as she is alive."

"But she doesn't have actual control of the business or the money?" Anna asked. "I wouldn't call that fair, Gino."

"Sharon has never worked a day in her life. She's happy being a lady of leisure. I guess her brother must have known that."

"Did she look happy?" Mary asked.

"I can't comment on that." Gino frowned. "But she didn't look surprised."

"What about Finn O'Malley?" Anna asked with bated breath.

"He gets an income for life too, like Sharon. Of course, his amount is nowhere close to hers. But he can live comfortably without having to get a job."

"So he didn't get Ruth's share." Julie summed up.

Gino shook his head.

"The will mentioned that Edward loved both his granddaughters equally. But Ruth had died without any offspring. He didn't think an outsider like O'Malley, however noble, should get half of the Gardiner fortune."

"That means Alison inherits everything!" Anna almost cut Gino off.

"Are you surprised?" he asked her.

"Not really, since this is the old will."

"What are you getting at, Anna?"

"We come back to the big announcement," Anna sighed. "What if Edward was planning to make a new will? All the secret meetings with the lawyers point to that. Alison would not have been the heir in that case."

"Are we certain Edward Gardiner didn't make a new will?" Julie questioned.

"The lawyers aren't aware of one," Gino told her.

"What if he was in a hurry?" Anna's eyes gleamed with excitement. "Couldn't he have written it out himself?"

"People do that all the time." Julie backed Anna. "I had an eccentric aunt who liked to dangle her meager fortune before her nieces and nephews like a carrot. She changed her will every month! Wrote it out herself and asked her maid and her neighbor to sign as witness."

"Edward had an army of people at his disposal," Gino argued.

"He was excited about something, though," Anna persisted. "Do you really think he couldn't have made a new will, Gino?"

"This is all speculation." Gino rubbed his forehead. "If Edward made a will, it must be somewhere in that house."

"Didn't the police search the Gardiner mansion?" Anna sat up. "What did they find?"

Gino offered to make some inquiries. He stepped away for a moment and placed a call. Anna watched him bob his head a few times and hang up shortly.

"You're in luck, Anna. That was the police chief. He's willing to let you go through what they found."

"That's a first," Julie smirked.

"The police haven't had much luck with the investigation. They thought O'Malley was involved because of the bags. But further scrutiny revealed many people had access to them. Now they are hesitating to pin the blame on Finn."

"Lack of evidence …" Julie nodded.

"What happens now?" Anna asked Gino.

"If you're free, you and I will go to the police station and look over some of the stuff they have."

Anna told him she was ready to leave immediately. Mary and Julie wished them luck. Gino called ahead to let the chief know they were on their way.

Leo was waiting for them inside the station. He led them to a small conference room. Anna noted the peeling gray paint on the walls and the lack of windows. She shuddered at the memory of being stuck in there.

A long table took up most of the space. Metal chairs were placed around it. Stacks of boxes were dumped on the table.

"This came from the Gardiner estate," Leo told them. "The chief said you can go through all of these papers. Just don't take anything outside this building."

"Thanks Leo," Anna said warmly. "Any thoughts on how to tackle these?"

"Why don't we each take a box? I have been assigned to help you and Uncle Gino."

Anna nodded gratefully. They discussed what they were looking for. Gino suggested taking a closer look at anything with Edward's signature.

"Let's set them aside," Anna agreed.

Two hours later, they sat back, exhausted. Their sorting had produced dozens of papers with the old man's signature on them but no will.

"If there's a second will, it's not here." Anna sighed. "I'm sorry this was such a waste of time, Gino."

"Have you ever considered Alison as a suspect?" Gino asked her. "What if she heard about the new will? Do you think she would harm her grandpa for money?"

"I think Alison was always the undisputed heir. Edward's wife is dead. So is his son. He might have split the money 50-50 between Ruth and Alison. But Ruth isn't alive either."

"Are we giving too much importance to the will?" Gino wondered. "Maybe money is not the motive here."

"According to town gossip, Finn blames Edward Gardiner for Ruth's death."

Gino looked sad.

"He's not the only one. Edward blamed himself. He thought Ruth and her child could have been saved at a city hospital. But Ruth insisted on giving birth at home."

"How depressing!" Anna thought of the two innocent lives that had been lost.

"I can't imagine Finn being underhanded. He's a soldier, Anna. He has a certain honor code."

"I won't argue with that. Who does that leave?"

"Sharon." Gino looked unconvinced.

"Can you be objective about her?"

"Of course I can, Anna. You don't know Sharon. She's a happy gal. I've never seen her say anything negative or bear a grudge against anyone."

"You mean she doesn't want for anything. So she couldn't have a motive to hurt her brother."

"Something like that."

"I want to believe you, Gino, but I need to be objective. Surely there must be something in Sharon's life that's less than ideal? I intend to find out."

Chapter 22

Anna sat in her living room, surrounded by friends and family.

"I love this time of year," she gushed happily. "And I love living in Dolphin Bay. There is an abundance of Christmas spirit wherever you look."

"You haven't lived anywhere else, Mom," Cassie reminded her. "But you're right. I had forgotten all about the Christmas market."

Every year, a host of stalls sprang up in the park that ran through the centre of Main Street. The holiday market offered a variety of foods, right from fancy cured meats, local artisanal cheeses, jams and jellies to fine chocolates. Gino's Mystic Hill winery had a stall there. So did the local knitting club. Ladies sold handmade quilts and pottery. There was plenty to tempt buyers armed with a holiday shopping list.

"How is it going with your Lights committee, Meg?" Sofia asked. "Any chances of winning the trophy this year?"

"We are hopeful, Nana. Everyone's been working very hard. You can see it all yourself in two days."

"We don't know what the other towns are doing," Julie warned. "Some of them are very competitive, Meg."

"I didn't care about winning at first." Meg was animated. "But I have slowly picked up on the excitement."

"Nothing wrong with that, Meg." Cassie took her side. "Especially at your age. That whole 'everyone is a winner' concept is a myth. You are either first or you aren't."

"It's a harsh life lesson," Anna nodded. "But I have to agree with Cassie."

"When is that young man of yours coming to dinner, Meg?" Sofia changed the subject.

"I'm not sure," Meg blushed. "Why does he have to come here, Nana?"

"So we can grill him about the important stuff!" Julie laughed. "What are you afraid of, kiddo?"

"Aren't you sure you like him?" Mary asked gently.

Gino had been quiet all this time. He set his wine glass down on a coaster and cleared his throat.

"Pardon me if I'm wrong, Meg. But I thought you liked Leo."

Meg blushed even more.

"Leo and I are friends. I look up to him."

"Is that code for something?" Gino frowned. "Do you think he's too old for you?"

"Leo's not going anywhere!" Julie shook her head. "Meg

needs to date a few kids before she gets serious about anyone."

Meg's face had been turning redder by the second. She excused herself and rushed to her room.

"Are you happy now?" Sofia clucked. "You made the poor child leave."

"Meg's tougher than you think, Nana," Cassie spoke up. "She'll be fine."

Julie and Mary left after that. Sofia bid them good night and went inside.

"I guess I should turn in too," Cassie winked. "Give you two love birds some alone time."

Anna suppressed a smile but didn't say anything. Cassie took the hint.

Gino patted the empty spot next to him on the couch. Anna didn't need an invitation. Gino put his arm around her and they sat quietly for some time, staring into the fire, enjoying each other's company.

"What's on your mind, cara?"

Anna looked up, surprised.

"You've never called me dear before."

"I've thought it." Gino took her hand in his. "I guess I was working up the courage to say it out loud."

"Gino Mancini! Are you telling me you are afraid of me?"

Gino twirled his mustache.

"I don't want to rush you, Anna. I know it hasn't been long since you lost John."

Anna was touched by Gino's concern.

"You are so kind, Gino. Honestly, John will always be in my heart. But I know how fleeting life can be. I want to embrace it fully."

"Good to know that," Gino smiled. "I can plan a special date for us now."

Anna promised she would look forward to it.

"So tell me," Gino prompted. "What's on your mind?"

"I was thinking about the holiday party at the Gardiners'. You know what struck me the most? They all seemed so happy. Everyone was smiling broadly, bursting with enthusiasm."

"That's how they were all the time," Gino said gravely. "I could always count on Edward to make me laugh."

"Would you say it was a happy household?"

"Very much so, Anna. I never saw them argue about anything either."

"What about enemies? Business rivals? Disgruntled employees?"

Gino shook his head.

"The Gardiners have always been hailed as great philanthropists. Edward continued the tradition. He could sense the slightest need of anyone around him. And he was ready to help in any way necessary."

"So he never denied anyone a raise, for example."

"The man I knew would never do that. All the employees at the Gardiner company got a 10% raise in their pay every year. Bonuses were extra."

"That does sound generous," Anna agreed grudgingly. "Growing up, I resented how much my father worshipped the Gardiners. I thought it was feudal, you know. But now I see why he looked up to them."

"You still don't sound convinced though. I have an idea. Why don't we go talk to Basil again?"

Anna gave a tiny shrug.

"I did get the feeling he knew more than he was telling. No harm in trying."

Gino promised to call the estate manager the next morning and fix an appointment with him.

"Time to leave, Anna. I have an early meeting with my manager tomorrow. But I should be free by lunch."

Anna woke up to a foggy morning. Bitterly cold winds tore through town that morning. The sun was finally beginning to peep through the clouds when Gino arrived at the café. They were meeting Basil before lunch.

He greeted them eagerly.

"How's your search going, Mrs. Butler? Any luck?"

"I'm having trouble with the motive. Everyone seems to have liked Edward Gardiner."

"He was like a guardian angel to many of us." Basil looked sad. "I already offered you my help. Please don't hesitate to ask me anything."

"What do you think of working for Alison?" Anna asked. "Isn't she kind of young to take over such a big company?"

"Alison was always the undisputed heir," Basil said. "The boss made it clear to everyone. He had been grooming Alison for the past five years. We knew she would take over the business one day."

"So the contents of the will didn't come as a surprise to you?" Gino probed.

Basil told them the will had never been secret.

"And Edward never got into a fight or disagreement with anyone in all these years?" Anna prodded. "He didn't lose his temper once?"

Anna saw a flicker of doubt flash through Basil's eyes.

"What is it?" She leaned forward in anticipation. "Don't leave anything out, however trivial."

"This was before my time," Basil began. "My father worked for the Gardiners too, you see. He used to talk about the big fight between Edward and his sister."

"You mean Sharon?" Anna confirmed.

"This is a bit delicate." Basil paused. "Very few people know about this, although there was some gossip in town at the time. Even the Gardiner money couldn't quash that."

"Does this have something to do with Pearson?" Anna tried to curb her excitement.

"So you found out? Sharon fell in love with George Pearson. They wanted to get married. Edward would have none of it, of course."

"Edward has always pampered Sharon and catered to every wish of hers," Gino mused. "I can't imagine him refusing her something."

"Everything but ..." Basil grimaced. "He belonged to a different generation. Can't blame him for that, I guess. All said and done, Pearson was their butler. The old man couldn't forget that."

"Couldn't they have gone away?" Anna cried. "Built a new life somewhere else?"

"Sharon did leave. So did Pearson. They came back a year later. My father told me Pearson had worked two jobs in the city, trying to make ends meet. But Sharon couldn't take it. She had lived in the lap of luxury all her life. Edward controlled all the money and he wanted her back."

"Pearson came back too?" Anna felt something didn't add up.

"The Gardiners needed a butler and Pearson was good at his job. Edward was ready to forgive and forget."

"And they lived happily ever after?" Anna caught Gino's eye and shook her head.

"This doesn't make sense, Basil." Gino twirled his mustache. "How could he let Pearson and Sharon live in the same house, knowing their history?"

"Something else happened that year." Basil scratched his sideburns with a pen. "Edward's son and his wife died in an accident."

"And he took it hard," Gino summed up. "I can see why he must have softened his stance toward Sharon."

They thanked Basil for his time and headed to Mystic Hill. Anna had agreed to have lunch with Gino.

"My cook makes the best enchilada pie," he told her. "I hope you're hungry."

"Can you imagine what a trial it must have been for Sharon and Pearson? Living under one roof without acknowledging their feelings?"

"Any man in his position would bear a massive grudge,"

Gino observed. "If Pearson hadn't died himself, he would be our number one suspect."

"Don't forget Sharon," Anna chided. "What do they say about revenge? That it's best served cold? What if the resentment she had suppressed all these years got out of hand?"

Chapter 23

Anna appreciated Gino's efforts to make her feel at home. The enchilada pie had been delicious. Dessert was chocolate cranberry biscotti with a fruit wine Gino wanted her to taste.

The day had turned colder but the roaring wood fire Gino lit added some cheer to the dreary atmosphere. Anna couldn't stop thinking of Sharon. Could the seemingly feather brained woman have harbored a lifelong hatred toward her brother?

"Am I boring you, Anna?" Gino's mustache twitched. "You haven't heard a word I said."

Gino's phone rang just then, saving Anna from an embarrassing moment.

Anna saw Gino's face harden as he listened to the voice at the other end.

"Bad news, I'm afraid."

Anna's thoughts flew to Cassie and Meg.

"It's about the Gardiners." Gino hastened to explain. "Forensics came back with the results. They matched the stuff they found on Edward with the bags from Finn's garage."

"That can't be good for him." Anna was dismayed.

"The police arrested him a few minutes ago," Gino sighed. "You won't like the next bit, Anna. I promised to help him if something like this happened."

"You're getting him a lawyer?" Anna prompted.

Gino nodded. He offered to drop Anna off at the café before going to the police station. The lawyer was going to meet him there and work on getting Finn out on bail.

The café was almost empty when Anna got there. She wondered how long it would take for news of Finn's arrest to spread through town.

Her fears were realized when a familiar scrawny figure swarmed in an hour later. Meg had just rushed off to meet some friends.

"We had a deal!"

Craig Rose jabbed a bony finger in her face. His mop of snowy white hair was in disarray. The ever present cardigan was unevenly buttoned.

"You promised to protect my boy, Mrs. Butler. You failed!"

"Wait a minute … the police found evidence against your boy. I can only do so much, Mr. Rose."

"Excuses, excuses! You failed, Madam. Don't expect me to help you now."

"You're being unfair." Anna's fists curled as she tried to control her emotions. "I have done everything I could to find out who killed Edward Gardiner."

Craig Rose was shaking his head vigorously.

"All I asked was …"

"And I made my stance very clear. I can only go after the truth. If Finn O'Malley is guilty, I am not going to help you hide it."

"Then our deal is off!" Craig Rose whirled around and started walking away.

"You can't leave just yet."

Anna hurried after the old man and barred the door.

"Tell me what you know about John. I've done my best to help Finn. Now it's your turn to honor your commitment."

"Not just yet," Craig Rose said shrewdly. "Are you sure you didn't miss any clues?" He grinned maliciously. "You think you are invincible, just like your husband."

Anna made up her mind.

"Let's go over to Finn's cottage. You are coming with me right now."

Craig took a deep breath and nodded.

"We can take my car, Mrs. Butler. Thanks."

Anna fumed silently on the way to the Gardiner estate. She was just humoring Craig Rose. She felt the chances of finding anything pertinent in Finn's cottage were slim to none. The police had obviously done a thorough search by this time.

"That's not the right attitude," Craig Rose nagged, almost reading her mind.

Anna looked at him guiltily.

"I'm sorry, what?"

"You have already made up your mind. You think this trip is a waste of time."

Anna assured him she would sincerely look for anything that might exonerate Finn O'Malley.

The cottage was deserted. Anna wondered what had happened to Chief. Someone from the main house must have taken him.

They spotted the tiny storage shed immediately. The door was wide open and a few loose papers fluttered outside on the breeze.

Anna looked around and found a big stack of poop bags. She pointed them out to Craig.

"That's the famous bag, used to kill Edward Gardiner."

"Finn O'Malley would not sneak up on anyone in the middle of the night. He is the kind that shoots an enemy point blank."

"Why do I keep hearing that?" Anna moaned. "He should not be shooting or stabbing anyone in any way. We are trying to prove he didn't do this, Mr. Rose."

A decrepit bench sat in the centre of the shed. Two cardboard boxes were dumped on it. Anna realized they were the source of the papers she had seen flying around.

"Let's go through these," she suggested.

"That looks like confidential stuff." Craig Rose was judgmental. "We don't want to pry."

"We also don't have a choice." Anna didn't hide her frustration. "I thought we are here to help Finn any way we can."

Craig Rose capitulated and started going through the papers. Anna set aside a hoard of bank and credit card statements. There were newspaper clippings about the war in Afghanistan. Assorted flyers and coupons for local garages, pet groomers and physical therapists. A stack of blue colored envelopes tied with a satin ribbon caught Anna's eye. She sniffed them curiously.

"Looks like scented paper."

"Those are private," Craig Rose snapped. "They are letters from Ruth. She wrote him regularly when he was posted in the war zone."

Anna hesitated before setting them aside. Ruth had been gone a long time. Anna decided it was safe to assume the letters would not help vindicate Finn.

"There's nothing here," she sighed. "Let's go through his cottage once."

Searching the cottage didn't take long. They were disappointed once again.

"Nothing much we can do here, I suppose," Craig Rose admitted reluctantly.

"It's like solving a puzzle," Anna explained. "Obviously, some pieces are still missing."

"You better find them soon then." Craig Rose stomped out after handing out his latest rebuke.

Anna decided to go for a walk after Craig Rose dropped her off in front of the café. She needed to clear her head. Half an hour later, she sat on a bench on the Coastal Walk, staring out at the dark blue waters of the bay. She was freezing in the cold, no closer to any fresh insights.

Anna was longing for a nap by the time she got home. Sofia fixed a hot toddy for her and sat on the edge of her bed.

"Don't you dare fall sick, Anna. Christmas is around the corner. And Gino and the girls are coming to dinner tonight."

"I'd forgotten all about that!" Anna sipped the warm drink. "Do we need to start cooking?"

"Everything's under control." Sofia stood up. "I decided to

keep it simple tonight. We are having chicken piccata with angel hair pasta and salad. Cassie's picking up sorbet from Paradise Market for dessert."

"We can all use a lighter meal, Mama," Anna nodded appreciatively.

Julie called later that evening, grumbling about being stuck in her story.

"I've been staring at a blank page for two hours, Anna."

"Take a break. Come have dinner with us. You can meet Meg's young man."

Phoenix had finally decided to accept Anna's invitation. Meg had been pacing the house nervously, begging them to go easy on him.

"Relax kiddo, it's just dinner." Cassie hadn't stopped grinning.

Anna and Meg were setting the table when the doorbell chimed. Gino stood outside, Phoenix just behind him. Julie's car pulled up.

Sofia sat in her chair, staring at Phoenix while the wine was poured and the antipasti platter passed around.

"You have an unusual name," she spoke up after taking a sip of the Riesling Gino had brought with him.

Phoenix had arrived empty handed, making him go down a notch in Anna's eyes. Not even a bunch of flowers, she thought dourly.

"Oh, Phoenix is not my real name," the youngster laughed. "That's just the name I go by at DBU."

Meg looked astonished.

"You never told me that! What is your actual name then?"

"Thomas Green." Phoenix laughed. "Can you imagine building any kinda street cred with a name like Tom Green? Sounds like some old fogey from the 1950s."

"What's wrong with the 1950s?" Sofia thundered. "I grew up in the 50s. It was a fine time."

"Beg your pardon," Phoenix sobered. "I didn't mean any disrespect."

"Where did you say you're from?" Julie intervened.

Her brow was set in a familiar frown. Anna braced herself for what Julie would say next.

"Blueberry Falls." Meg looked at Phoenix grimly. "Unless you made that up too."

"Of course not, Meg!" Phoenix looked around smugly. "I'm from Blueberry Falls alright. Born and raised."

"Are you related to Isabella Green?" Julie asked casually. "I think she lives in Blueberry Falls."

"She's the mayor of Blueberry Falls." Phoenix beamed proudly. "She's my mother."

"What?" Meg sprang up. "The same Blueberry Falls that is our biggest rival in the Seaside Christmas Lights contest?"

"I guess." Phoenix gave a noncommittal shrug.

"Is that why you strung me along?" Meg shrieked. "I should've known better."

All eyes in the room were on Meg.

"Did I say something wrong?" Phoenix looked mystified.

Julie stood up and put a hand on his shoulder.

"I think you should leave now, sweetie. Meg will call you later."

Phoenix looked at Meg, seeking confirmation. She folded her arms and looked away.

"You folks have a good evening," Phoenix mumbled before walking out.

Julie shut the door behind him and turned around.

"What was all that, Meg?" Anna asked sharply. "That's no way to treat a guest." She whirled around and stared at Julie. "You should know better!"

"Don't you see what just happened here?" Julie flung up her arms in despair. "That kid was taking advantage of Meg."

"How?" Anna, Cassie and Sofia chorused.

"He was spying on us," Meg declared. "He wanted to know about our theme for the contest, Anna. That's why he pretended to like me."

Meg stood up with a sob and ran to her room.

Chapter 24

Anna and the Firecrackers sat in a window booth at the Tipsy Whale. They had just ordered lunch.

"The cookie exchange takes place tomorrow." Anna licked her lips, relishing the spicy flavor of the mulled cider she was drinking. "I still need to bake a couple dozen cookies."

"We have a good selection this time," Mary hummed. "Should we be eating all this sugar?"

"Live it up while you can," Julie said. "We can go on a juice fast in January."

"Just like every year, you mean?" Anna asked.

The three friends burst into peals of laughter.

None of them had ever been successful in sticking to a diet. Mary's husband was a gourmand who loved rich food. Anna's husband John had been a connoisseur of the local seafood and the fresh homemade pasta she often cooked for him. Julie had the least temptation, living alone, but she was a stress eater. She was used to snacking on junk food during her writing sprints.

"How's Meg?" Julie asked. "Planning to go bash up that thug?"

"Aren't you being hard on Phoenix?" Anna quizzed. "You

don't believe he could fall for a sweet girl like Meg?"

"He could," Julie nodded. "But I bet he didn't. Wait till you hear what Sally said."

"You told Sally about this?" Anna was aghast. "Meg's going to be mortified."

"She has no reason to feel guilty." Julie plunged ahead. "He preyed on her."

"What if Blueberry Falls copies our ideas?" Mary asked.

"Sally said it's too late for us now," Julie told them. "We can't change our theme at this hour. Everything is set out and rigged up for the inauguration tonight."

"Why can't we lodge a complaint against Blueberry Falls?" Anna asked. "Have them disqualified?"

"There's no proof," Julie shot Anna down. "Sally doesn't want to give them the satisfaction."

Their food arrived. The daily special was a hearty meatless burger made with walnuts and brown rice. It was topped with velvety melted Monterey Jack cheese from the region. Murphy, the pub owner came over to greet them.

"How do you like those beer caramelized onions?" he beamed at them.

"Good job, Murph!" Julie gave him a thumbs up and dabbed her mouth with a napkin. "And the blue cheese is just right too."

"Finn O'Malley talked me into having a meatless special every week. Seemed like a good bloke. Who'd have thunk, huh?"

"You think he's guilty?" Anna probed.

"The police think so," Murphy said, wiping some spilled sauce with a rag. "They wouldn't take the trouble of arresting him if they didn't have proof."

"Isn't he charming?" Julie smirked after Murphy had moved on to another table.

"What do you say, Anna?" Mary asked. "I hope you haven't given up."

"Murphy may be right." Anna took a bite of her burger and gave a tiny shrug. "The police aren't completely dumb."

"You can't be saying that!" Julie protested. "I thought you believed in Finn."

"Unfortunately, the evidence points to Finn O'Malley. He had a motive and he was free to enter the main house any time he wanted. So he had the opportunity."

"Do you really believe he hated the old man?" Julie asked.

"Gino and I were talking about it," Anna nodded. "Edward could have insisted Ruth give birth at a hospital. But he caved. Finn blames him for not being firm. And I agree. Edward should have exhibited better judgment."

Julie didn't look convinced.

"Sometimes, things are exactly how they seem. I think we should leave the Gardiners to fend for themselves. This was supposed to be a happy time for us."

"It still is," Mary consoled her. "But I agree with you, Anna. You did all you could."

Anna ate the last couple of fries on her plate and smiled wanly. She felt like she was throwing Finn O'Malley under the bus.

"I have an idea!" Julie's eyes gleamed with excitement. "How about taking a little road trip? It's the perfect way to indulge in some holiday cheer."

Anna and Mary glanced at each other.

"This can't be good," they chorused.

They piled into Julie's big SUV five minutes later. Julie cranked the heat up high but refused to tell them where they were going. They merged on the Pacific Coast Highway some time later.

"Are we going to San Francisco?" Mary asked from the back seat.

"Is this an impromptu shopping trip, Julie?" Anna echoed.

Julie told them to be patient. She took an exit some time later, making Anna groan.

"Blueberry Falls? Why are we going to Blueberry Falls?"

"We are doing some recce."

"What does that mean?" Anna scrunched up her face. "I've never done that before."

"Everything is fair when it comes to winning the Christmas Lights contest … or whatever they call it."

"We are going to spy on them." Mary shook her head. "I don't know if I approve, Julie."

"We're just going to hang out, girls," Julie consoled them. "Act like any other tourist. Do some window shopping, check out any special holiday markets they have, chat with the locals, maybe even get some ice cream."

"And if we manage to get a glimpse of their lights while doing this, or hear someone talk about them, it's not really our fault." Anna caught on. "I like this plan."

"Well, when you put it that way …" Mary capitulated.

The town of Blueberry Falls was packed with visitors and Julie barely found a spot in the temporary parking lot.

"Just look at all these people!" Mary exclaimed. "Dolphin Bay never attracts so many tourists. What are they doing that we aren't?"

Julie pointed toward a medium built woman with wavy auburn hair. She wore a festive red coat with a holiday themed scarf wound around her neck. Glittery reindeer dangled from her ears. A younger woman followed her around with a tiny notepad in her hand. Another woman carried a large bag stuffed with tiny gaily wrapped packages.

The woman greeted the people she encountered and talked and laughed with them. Every person got a tiny gift from the large bag.

"She's coming here," Julie hissed.

They all pasted smiles on their faces.

"Hello! Welcome to Blueberry Falls. I'm Isabella Green, the mayor. We are so happy to have you here."

She asked if they were looking for anything in particular. Julie gave a vague answer. Isabella pointed out some of the popular shops and advocated the holiday market.

"You should come around tomorrow evening. We put up a lavish display of lights on the beach. Our town always wins the local prize for it."

"That's interesting," Mary said. "Do you have giant Santas and reindeers? I saw a display like that once."

Isabella giggled and leaned forward.

"It's all hush hush. The Lights Committee will have my head if I let anything slip."

Isabella Green bid them a good day and walked on.

"That's why they have so many visitors!" Julie smirked. "Their mayor is nice and friendly. Unlike Lara Crawford!"

"She did seem pleasant," Anna mused. "So Phoenix is her son, huh? I can see the resemblance."

"Do you believe her boy was duping our Meg all this time?" Mary asked.

"Phoenix is a bit odd." Anna paused. "But I think he really likes Meg."

They walked around Blueberry Falls and shopped for some knickknacks. Anna bought some handmade jewelry a little girl was selling. Julie did her best to learn more about the lights. Finally, they decided it was time to go home when they watched the sun hug the horizon.

Back home, Anna was so exhausted she barely spoke to anyone. Sofia and Meg were both in a reflective mood and Cassie spent the evening chatting with Bobby on the phone.

They had leftovers for dinner and Anna retired early. She fell into a deep sleep immediately and woke up with a start a few hours later. The electric clock by her bedside showed it was just a few minutes past midnight.

Anna yawned and rubbed her eyes, dragging herself to the kitchen. She made herself some herbal tea and sat at the table, sipping the hot, comforting brew. The memory of the last days spent with her husband niggled her mind. She wondered what Craig Rose was withholding. The chances of finding it out were beginning to look slim. Anna thought he was getting meaner by the day.

Anna had a sudden yearning to see John's face. She went back to her bedroom to look for her phone and pulled up some old pictures.

Anna's eyes filled with tears as she flipped through the

photo gallery on her phone. After a while, the image on the screen barely registered as a lifetime of memories overwhelmed her. A peculiar symbol nagged her and she swiped through the photos again to pull it up.

Anna stared at the picture that had bothered her. It belonged on an empty envelope she had found in the box of papers in Finn's storage shed. The crest like graphic had seemed familiar to her at the time but she couldn't place it. She had snapped a picture of the envelope, deciding to look into it later. Anna still couldn't remember where she had seen it before.

Anna gave up trying to jog her memory and picked up a book. She fell asleep some time later, no closer to any fresh insights into the envelope.

Chapter 25

Anna felt antsy the next morning. She had fallen into a troubled sleep, waking up with a start when her alarm went off. A long hot shower hadn't helped much.

Meg was in the kitchen, stacking cookies in a large container.

"I made stacks of a dozen cookies and wrapped them in plastic, just like you asked, Anna."

"The cookie exchange!" Anna exclaimed. "I totally forgot."

"Don't worry," Meg assured her. "We're all set. The ladies are meeting by the gazebo at two this afternoon."

Anna started mixing cake batter as Meg prattled on. They rushed through breakfast before loading the van and heading to the café.

A bunch of customers stood on the sidewalk, waiting for their coffee and pastries.

"I think opening the café an hour early was a good idea, Meg."

Anna fortified herself with sips of coffee as she served the customers. She was finally beginning to feel alert as the caffeine kicked in. The day promised to be a whirlwind of activity. Anna decided to go for a walk and get some fresh air as soon as the crowd thinned.

She was pulling on her coat when a familiar figure pushed the door open and breezed in, smelling faintly of roasted chestnuts.

"This is a surprise." Anna greeted Craig Rose, knowing she sounded acerbic.

Craig Rose shivered in his cardigan and waved a piece of paper at her.

"You better see this."

Anna reluctantly took off her coat and looked around for a place to sit. The café was packed. She ushered him through the connecting arch to the bookstore. They sat at a long table next to large windows overlooking the bay.

Craig placed the paper on the table and pushed it toward Anna.

"What's this?" Anna scanned the paper quickly. "Is this some kind of DNA report? Where did you find this, Mr. Rose?"

"In Finn's storage shed. I couldn't stop thinking that we might have missed something. So I went back there."

Anna stared at the peculiar logo on the letterhead of the report. It matched the one on the envelope. She still couldn't place where she had seen it.

"This says Edward cannot be Alison's grandfather. There is

only a 12% match between their DNA. But this makes no sense. What is the meaning of this?"

Craig Rose leaned back in his chair.

"You are the sleuth. Why don't you find out?"

"You're right," Anna stood up. "In the meantime, why don't you work on what you're going to tell me?"

Anna didn't wait for Craig's reaction. She walked out into the street and started walking toward the Coastal Walk, eagerly breathing in the cool, salty air.

Fifteen minutes later, Anna was back in the café with a clear plan of action. She stood before the fireplace and rubbed her hands to warm them up. Then she placed a call to Gino.

Gino had just been about to call her. Finn O'Malley had been released on bail the previous evening. They agreed to go visit him. Gino picked her up half an hour later.

Anna voiced what she was thinking on the drive to the Gardiner estate.

"Did you ever suspect this?"

Gino shook his head.

"But Finn must have, since it was found in his things. Be patient, Anna. We'll get to the bottom of this soon enough."

Gino parked outside the main house and they started

walking down the path to Finn's cottage. Anna hoped they would find him at home.

Finn was playing with Chief outside the cottage, throwing a ball for him to fetch. His face broke into a smile when he saw them.

"Aren't you cold?" Anna asked curiously.

Finn was dressed in his usual white tee shirt and camo pants.

He shrugged and led them inside. Anna got to the point. She showed him the piece of paper Craig Rose had given her.

"Do you know what this is?"

"Where did you find this?" he asked.

"We had to go through your things." Anna was apologetic. "We didn't mean to pry."

"I appreciate your efforts," Finn said shyly. "But I'm not sure what this is. I can guess though."

Gino gave him an encouraging smile.

"What are you thinking, son?"

Chief had come in with them and was sitting by Finn's feet. Finn stroked the dog's fur and tried to gather his thoughts.

"Alison doesn't like me. I don't know why."

Gino and Anna said nothing, waiting for the soldier to continue.

"Maybe she thought Ruth married beneath her." Finn shrugged. "I don't know. And I didn't really care. But then I came to live here. She made it very clear she didn't approve."

"Did you feel the same way?" Anna asked.

"She was Ruth's sister. That was enough for me, you know. But then I started noticing some things."

"About what?" Gino prompted.

"I go to the Tipsy Whale for a drink once in a while," Finn began. "People in Dolphin Bay love the Gardiners. They are all so friendly and they have done a lot for the region. So you rarely hear anything bad about them."

"But …" Anna nudged.

"I was sitting in a booth by myself when Sharon came in to pick up some sandwiches. Two old timers sitting somewhere behind me started talking about her. To be honest, I was kind of preoccupied, feeling sorry for myself. I wouldn't have noticed what they were saying. But they started talking about Sharon's past. I got the shock of my life."

"Let me guess…" Anna gave Gino a knowing look. "They mentioned Sharon's affair with Pearson?"

Finn was astonished.

"According to them, it was much more than that. They seemed to be in Pearson's camp. Thought Sharon used him and dumped him because he wasn't as rich as her."

"Did you confront Sharon?" Gino was curious.

Finn shook his head. "I barely thought about it. Then Alison came here one day to pick a fight with me. It was silly. But something clicked in my mind. I thought of how much she resembled Pearson."

"We're talking about the same Alison, right?" Anna interrupted. "Emerald green eyes, left dimple, golden hair?"

"She does look like the Gardiners at first glance," Finn nodded. "But you'll notice how much she's like Pearson if you look closely."

"So you thought Sharon and Pearson had a child and that child was Alison?" Gino didn't look convinced. "That sounds like quite a stretch, son."

"That's what I thought two days later after my big aha moment." Finn looked sheepish. "But I decided to see it through. I got some samples from Alison and Edward and sent them to a lab for analysis."

"I'm guessing you did this without their knowledge?" Anna raised an eyebrow questioningly.

"Don't ask me how I did it." Finn shrugged. "But it was all for nothing. I never got a look at that report."

Anna was trying to make sense of everything she knew.

"I found an empty envelope with that peculiar logo in your storage shed, Finn. And this report contains the same logo so it must have been in that envelope at some point."

"That report went missing," Finn told them. "This is the first time I'm looking at this."

"According to this report, Alison cannot be Edward's granddaughter," Anna mused. "She's not a strong match so she can't be his son's daughter. But she does share some DNA with him. She could be Sharon's, I guess."

"None of it matters now," Finn sighed. "Ruth's gone. So is Edward. Alison is not keen on my staying here."

"You have a long life ahead of you." Gino placed his hand on Finn's shoulder. "It's time to plan your next steps."

They said goodbye to Finn and walked back to Gino's truck. Anna had a strong hunch. She tried to curb her excitement and took Gino's arm in hers.

"Can you talk to the police chief again? I want to look at the stuff they brought back from the main house."

"What are you thinking, Anna?" Gino humored her.

"I might be on to something. But I'd rather confirm it before I say anything out loud."

"Can this wait?" Gino smiled. "I was thinking of taking you to that taco place for lunch."

Anna's pained expression said it all. Gino caved and soon they were back in the tiny conference room at the police station. Anna looked for the box that had come from Edward's study. She rifled through the papers until she found one with the now familiar logo.

"I knew it!" she exclaimed. "This has been tormenting me for days."

Gino quickly read the paper Anna held.

"This is the same report we just gave Finn. But this looks like a copy."

"Don't you see?" Anna's eyes glittered. "This means Edward knew the truth about Alison."

Gino's mouth tightened as he processed what Anna said.

"Question is, who told him?"

Chapter 26

Anna placed her lunch order and looked around her in dismay. The Yellow Tulip Diner was bursting at the seams.

"We can't talk here, Gino," she cried.

"Good." Gino gave his own order to the waitress and handed her the menu. "You're buzzing like a bee, Anna. You need to calm down. Take a break from your sleuthing."

A group of ladies waved at Anna and she reluctantly waved back, pasting a fake smile on her face.

"I forgot all about the cookie exchange," she moaned. "I think I'm going to miss it this year."

She fired off a couple of messages.

"Meg has to go somewhere. She sounded very mysterious. Maybe Cassie or Mama can step in."

The waitress set a platter of steaming burgers and crisp crinkle cut fries before them, along with Anna's root beer float.

Anna took a bite of the burger and found she was hungry. She didn't come up for air until she had finished it. The fries came next. Anna was dunking a bunch of fries in ketchup when she realized Gino was smiling at her.

"Why are you looking at me like that?" she asked.

"You're adorable." Gino grinned. "What do you want for dessert?"

They decided to share the berry pie.

Anna ignored the looks they got and held Gino's hand as they walked out of the diner.

"So Mr. Police Chief," Anna teased. "Where do you think we are going next?"

Gino scratched his head and beamed at her.

"The Gardiner mansion, to meet Sharon."

"Bingo!" Anna laughed.

Gino cranked up the radio on their way back to the Gardiner estate. Anna sang along with it, in a good mood. She felt she was close to discovering what had happened to Edward Gardiner.

"Let's hope Sharon isn't out shopping."

"Do you think she'll own up to what happened all those years ago?" Gino asked.

"Edward's gone," Anna pointed out. "And so is Pearson. Sharon should jump at the chance of reuniting with her daughter."

Sharon opened the door herself. If she was surprised to see

them, she didn't show it.

"Hermes is having a big sale in the city," she told Anna as they sat in the living room. "It's invite only. Starts in three hours."

"This shouldn't take long, Sharon." Gino took the lead. "We came across some surprising information today. Something you have been hiding for many years."

Sharon's green eyes blinked.

"How did you find out?"

Anna gave her a brief account of what they had learned from Finn.

"We are trying to establish how the DNA report reached Edward. Did you give it to him, Sharon?"

Sharon laughed mirthlessly.

"Why would I do that? I kept Alison's parentage secret for so many years, I almost forgot she was my own daughter."

Anna sensed she wasn't done.

"Did Pearson know about her?" she asked gently.

Sharon's eyes glistened.

"He didn't. I hid it well, you know. Neither Edward nor Pearson had an inkling. That's why George was so mad when he found out."

"Did he steal the report from Finn?" Gino asked.

"George went over to the cottage with a message for Finn. The envelope was lying right there. He saw it was from a DNA lab. Curiosity got the better of him."

"But the report doesn't say anything about you," Anna pointed out.

"The report said Alison was not Edward's granddaughter." Sharon stifled a sob. "George came to me with the report because he thought I might be able to make some sense out of it." Her eyes begged them to understand. "You see, I was the one who brought Alison home all those years ago, just after her parents were killed in an accident."

"No one suspected you?" Gino asked.

Sharon shook her head. "I could have lied again. Told George my nephew adopted Alison. Steve and Suzie had talked about adoption a lot."

"But you'd had enough." Anna finished for her. "You wanted the truth to come out."

"I did George a grave injustice. The guilt had been eating at me for years. I told him everything."

"Did you expect him to keep it quiet?" Gino looked thoughtful.

Sharon blew her nose in a tissue.

"I didn't think that far. But his reaction surprised me. He

was mad at me, of course. We had a big fight. Then he copied the report and gave it to my brother. He wanted to rub it in."

"Edward always had good things to say about Pearson." Gino twirled his mustache. "He boasted about how loyal the butler had been to the Gardiners."

"When George and I wanted to get married, Edward opposed us with all his might. No one knew I was pregnant. George and I went away, presumably in a sulk. George worked two low paying jobs in another town while I stayed with Steve. We didn't even see each other during that time. Then Edward and George reached some kind of truce. When I came back with the baby, George treated me like a stranger."

"That must have been hard on you," Anna commiserated.

"Frankly, I was in a daze. I handed the baby over to my sister-in-law and went back to being a ditzy socialite, someone who only cared about parties and pretty dresses."

"You and Pearson never rekindled your feelings for each other?" Anna was surprised.

Sharon blushed.

"Not for a long time. Edward was always present as a deterrent. Two years ago, I asked George if we could be friends again."

Anna could guess what Sharon was leaving unsaid. Unfortunately, with Pearson gone, her story would never have a happy ending.

"What happened when Pearson told your brother about Alison?" Gino tried to steer the conversation back on track.

"Edward was in shock. George told him it was poetic justice. He had kept us apart cruelly but ended up raising our daughter as his own."

"Was this the big announcement Edward kept referring to?" Anna asked. "He must have decided to cut Alison off."

"On the contrary," Sharon chuckled. "Edward sought me out. He told me he would always love Alison as his own. She was still the heir to the Gardiner fortune. Nothing would change that."

"So what was the surprise he kept alluding to?" Gino asked urgently. "I strongly believe it got him killed."

"He wouldn't tell me." Sharon was looking tired. "He just said it was a miracle worthy of Christmas."

"Does Alison know she's your daughter?" Anna watched Sharon's reaction.

Sharon shook her head. She had a yearning look in her eyes.

Gino stood up and gave Anna a knowing look.

"We need to talk to Alison, Sharon. Where can we find her?"

The doorbell rang at that moment, startling them. Sharon

stood up and stalked out of the room. Anna followed her after a split second. Gino was right behind.

The massive front door was wide open and a middle aged couple stood outside. Sharon's face was white, her mouth hanging open in shock.

The man came forward when he saw Gino and offered him a hand.

"Are you Gino Mancini? You used to come around here a lot with your papa."

Sharon's knees buckled at that very moment and Gino caught her deftly before she hit the ground.

An hour later, Gino steered his truck out of the Gardiner estate while he drove Anna home. Anna was trying to come to terms with the bizarre turn of events.

"My mind's reeling," she sighed. "I can't even imagine what Sharon's feeling right now."

The mystery couple had turned out to be Steven and Suzie Gardiner. Edward's son and his wife had narrowly escaped losing their lives. They had been on their way to some remote place in Africa to work as aid workers. Steven and his wife met someone they knew and accepted a ride with them. As fate would have it, the bus they were supposed to travel on met with an accident. Not a single body had been found and they were declared dead based on the passenger list.

"Why did they never get in touch with the family?" Anna asked Gino.

"Steven had no interest in the family business. He dreamed of working with indigenous tribes in Africa and South America. Edward's attitude toward Sharon and Pearson shocked him. Sharon was more a sister to him than an aunt. He decided to cut the cord and disappear. He says he mailed a note telling the family where he was going, but I don't think Edward ever got it. When Steven didn't hear back from him, he thought Edward had disowned him or something."

"What about Ruth?" Anna's eyebrows shot up. "She was their daughter, right?"

"They knew the jungles of Africa were no place for a child. He trusted his mother to take care of her."

"Why come back after all these years?" Anna quizzed. "Ruth's gone anyway."

"Steven didn't know that when he contacted his father. He wasn't sure if he would be welcome."

"The old man must have been overjoyed." Anna thought of how ecstatic she had been when she first met Meg.

"Edward wanted them home for Christmas." Gino sounded sad. "It would have been a big surprise for everyone."

"Do you believe Steven didn't know about Edward's death?" Anna asked.

"They were traveling on a cargo ship for the past few weeks." Gino shrugged. "No one knew they were coming so who was going to tell them?"

"You know what this means, Gino?" Anna expelled a deep breath.

Gino's face was grim.

"I'm going to meet the police chief as soon as I drop you home, Anna."

Chapter 27

Anna tucked into the olive and red pepper omelet she had cooked for breakfast. The three cheeses she had added gave it a robust flavor.

"The smoked gouda tastes really good, Anna," Sofia praised.

Meg and Cassie murmured their approval. Their faces were lit up with megawatt smiles.

"What's up with you two?" Anna picked up her avocado toast.

"Cassie's happy because Bobby arrives tomorrow. She can't wait to get all the latest Hollywood gossip from him."

Cassie elbowed Meg and made a face at her.

"Meg's grinning like a cat because she had a hot date last night."

"Date?" Anna and Sofia chorused.

"Are we still talking about Phoenix?" Anna teased. "Or did you go out with someone else?"

"Phoenix and I made up," Meg said shyly.

"And how did that happen?" Sofia wanted to know. "Did that boy admit to spying on you?"

"He wasn't spying on me, Nana." Meg was sheepish. "I told him why I was mad at him. He said he started coming around to the café because he couldn't stop thinking of me. The Lights contest had nothing to do with it."

"And you believed him?" Cassie smirked.

"He said he would do anything to convince me otherwise. We went to Blueberry Falls. I met his mom. She was very nice to me."

"The girls and I ran into her," Anna nodded. "She is quite friendly."

"Phoenix showed me their plans for the lights and even took me to the beach. He let me peep under the displays."

"No harm done," Cassie remarked. "You weren't going to replicate them in a day."

"All he wanted to show me was their display was nothing like ours," Meg said stoutly. "And it isn't. In fact, they couldn't be more different."

"The contest was kicked off yesterday, Meg. I don't think either town can make any changes now. So you should stop worrying about the lights."

"You're right, Anna." Meg giggled. "I thought the same. Phoenix and I strolled around Blueberry Falls, taking in their display. Then we came here and checked out the Coastal Walk."

"So you're giving him a second chance," Anna smiled. "That's kind of you, Meg."

"Phoenix is fun to hang out with," Meg began. "But I'm not sure I feel anything more for him."

"That's okay, kid," Cassie said. "That's what the first few dates are for, getting to know each other."

"The cookie exchange was a big success," Sofia declared. "Everyone loved your cranberry white chocolate cookies, Anna. Mary and I drove to the children's home and handed over the ones we collected for them."

"I did some last minute shopping," Cassie shared. "I think I'm finally done."

The kitchen door flew open, bringing in a few drops of rain. Gino wiped his feet on the mat and came in. Anna was glad he had stopped ringing the doorbell and was finally using the back door like her friends.

Anna could barely hold her excitement.

"She did it, Anna." Gino looked crushed. "Alison confessed to both murders. She killed Edward and Pearson."

A collective gasp went up through the room.

"Was Rupert involved?" Meg jumped down from her stool and stared at Gino. "He never hid how happy he was about Mr. Gardiner's death."

"He wasn't," Gino told her. "Alison did it all by herself."

"But why?" Sofia cried. "Why would that girl kill her grandpa?"

"He wasn't her grandpa, Mama," Anna said. "We found that out yesterday."

"Wait a minute, Mom." Cassie held up a hand. "This is too confusing. Why don't you let Gino tell us everything from the beginning?"

Anna fixed a breakfast plate for Gino and watched him eat a few bites.

"Anna and I had quite a day yesterday," he began.

He told them about the DNA report and the truth about Alison's birth. There was another gasp when he told them about Steven and Suzie.

"I went and talked to the police chief after I dropped Anna home last night."

"What made you suspect Alison?" Meg asked, wide eyed.

"Unfortunately, she was the only one left." Gino sighed. "It had to be her by the process of elimination. Edward and Pearson were gone. The evidence against Finn was shaky and I didn't believe his motive was strong enough. The same applied to Sharon. She might have borne a grudge but we saw how she broke down yesterday. She's the biggest victim in this whole saga. And Pearson was too, I guess."

"What was Alison's motive?" Cassie questioned.

"Alison is hungry for power and money. She wanted total control of the Gardiner empire. She was capable of anything if her position was threatened."

"Is that why she did it, Gino?" Anna asked quietly. "Did she own up to it?"

Gino pushed his plate away and took a sip of orange juice.

"Alison learnt everything the wrong way. She almost walked in on Pearson and Edward when they were talking about her birth. It shattered every belief she had. Being the butler's daughter meant she had no claim on the estate."

"But she was Sharon's daughter too!" Anna exclaimed. "With Ruth gone, she was the next of kin anyway."

"She didn't know that," Gino explained. "Sadly enough, she never heard the part about Sharon being her mother. She was already on edge when Edward started talking about the big announcement. Alison was sure he was going to cut her out of his will and give everything to Finn."

"So she was already plotting something at the time of the holiday party?" Anna remembered how much Edward had doted on Alison.

"She dropped some hints about taking over the business," Gino told them. "If Edward had openly declared he was handing over everything to her, she might have spared him."

"But he kept talking about that big announcement," Cassie murmured.

"Edward had no doubts about who would succeed him," Gino continued. "He and his wife raised Alison since she was a baby. She was the undisputed heir. Knowing him as I did, I think Pearson's words might have made an impact too. It really was ironic, raising the child of a union he had forbidden."

"What about Finn?" Anna asked. "Where does he come in?"

"Finn was never interested in the business. He's just a lonely man who missed his wife. Edward was like a father figure to him. But Alison never believed that."

"Did she use the poop bags to frame Finn?" Anna's mouth hung open.

"Alison planned everything carefully. She used the plastic bags from Finn's storage shed, knowing forensics would find a match. She was confident the announcement was a new will. She wanted to get Edward out of the way before that."

"And Pearson?" Cassie asked. "He was her biological father, wasn't he?"

"He was the butler, the hired help. She didn't want to be associated with him."

"That's cruel." Meg looked stricken.

Cassie put an arm around her shoulders to comfort her.

"Did she overhear something again?" Sofia wanted to know. "Was this Pearson going to publicly claim her as his daughter?"

"That's what she was afraid of," Gino nodded. "She thought Sharon might contest the will once she learned that Alison was Pearson's daughter."

"But Sharon would never have done that!" Anna sighed. "So Alison had no idea who her mother was? Didn't she ever wonder?"

"She never got past the shock of being the butler's daughter." Gino massaged his temples. "I've known her since she was a babe, Anna. Held her in my arms, given her piggyback rides. How could she turn out like this?"

"Did anyone tell her about Sharon?" Anna closed her eyes, feeling sorry for the woman.

"They told her, Anna." Gino said softly. "That's when she broke down and confessed."

"What about Steven and Suzie?" Anna wanted to know. "They got a series of shocks. I wonder how they are coping with all this."

"They are going back to Africa," Gino told her. "There's nothing to hold them here."

"And the Gardiner fortune?" Anna asked. "Who's going to take care of it now?"

"Alison is still the heir. Turns out Steven and Suzie adopted her legally when she was born. Whether you think of her as their daughter or Sharon's daughter, she inherits everything.

My guess is Sharon will start taking an interest in the business."

"She needs a fresh purpose," Anna agreed. "I think she will manage everything admirably. She's a Gardiner, after all."

"Does this mean you are done with your sleuthing, Anna?" Sofia demanded imperiously.

"Yes Mama."

"Good," Sofia grunted. "Christmas is almost upon us. There's work to be done, girl."

Epilogue

It was Christmas Eve. Anna had mixed feelings as she walked to Bayside Books. The bookstore and café were closed for a week. Anna thought it was the perfect place for a clandestine meeting with Craig Rose.

Her heart fluttered a bit as she thought of what she was going to learn. Part of her was sure that Craig Rose would have nothing. He had just been stringing her along. The other part dreaded the secrets he would reveal.

Anna squared her shoulders and enjoyed the bracing weather. The sun had come out to bathe Dolphin Bay in a pale, watery light. The freezing air stung her cheeks, making her feel alive. It was as close to a white Christmas as they would get in Dolphin Bay.

Anna tried to focus on the good things that had happened in the past few days. Cassie's friend Bobby had arrived. He had charmed Sofia in five minutes. Bobby had promised he would spare them any talk of diet or exercise until after the holidays. He regaled them with scandalous stories of his rich and famous clients, sending everyone into peals of laughter. Meal times and evenings had become a joyous affair.

The Firecrackers had gone to San Francisco for their last shopping trip of the season. Anna had picked up the custom earrings she had ordered for Meg, Cassie and herself. Her husband John had gifted her a diamond bracelet when Cassie was born. She had taken the stones from that bracelet and combined them with each of their birthstones in a new setting. She hoped the girls would like having a memento to remember John.

Gino had taken her out for a special date as promised. They drove to an exclusive seafood restaurant a few miles south of town. It was a romantic night and Anna had been surprised by how much she enjoyed herself.

The sun disappeared behind a cluster of black clouds. Anna stood on the sidewalk under the magnolia tree, fishing in her purse for her keys. She had come early on purpose. She needed time to prepare herself.

The bells behind the door jangled just as the coffee started brewing. Craig Rose came in, wearing his favorite red cardigan. The smug sneer Anna was used to seeing on his face was gone. Instead, he appeared inscrutable.

Craig declined her offer of coffee. Anna cupped her hands around her mug, trying to find some comfort in the warmth seeping through. Was she finally going to learn what had happened to her beloved husband?

"I owe you an apology." Craig cleared his throat. "A big one." He stared at her with eyes laden with remorse. "What can I say? I haven't been myself since I lost my son. The grief must have addled my brain."

Anna saw a man who was suffering. She decided to forget how harshly he had treated her.

"I lost someone dear too."

"Finn O'Malley was kind to me. I latched on to him like a lifeline. The thought of losing him was unbearable."

Anna wished Craig Rose would hurry. Did he even know anything about John?

Craig Rose must have sensed her impatience. He stopped midsentence and sighed.

"I have bothered you enough already, Mrs. Butler. Anna. Let's talk about why we are here."

He leaned forward and began speaking in a hushed tone.

"I think your husband was murdered, Mrs. Butler. He didn't die naturally."

"I already knew that!" Anna blurted. "Aren't you going to tell me about his affair?"

"What affair?" Craig Rose was looking bewildered.

"There has been some talk," Anna explained. "John was seeing another woman before he died. I thought you were going to tell me about her."

"I'm sorry to hear that." Craig sounded sincere. "But I barely knew your husband. Why would I know anything about his extramarital activities?"

"Then what do you know?" Anna cried.

Anna feared her hopes were about to be dashed again.

"I overheard something," Craig began. "It didn't mean much to me at the time. I didn't connect the dots until all those rumors about you killing your husband started flying around town."

Anna gulped.

"Don't worry," Craig assured her. "We don't run in the same circles, but I knew you by reputation. In my opinion, you have an impeccable character. So I never believed what they were saying about you."

"What did you overhear?" Anna prompted, afraid Craig would launch into another monologue.

"You know I own a wine shop in town? It's right behind Paradise Market."

Anna nodded.

"This was over two years ago so my memory isn't very clear. A couple of young men came into the store. I think they were planning a party. They bought several bottles of every kind of liquor and ordered two kegs of beer. That's why I remember them."

Anna forced herself to breathe normally.

"I was wiping down shelves in the adjoining aisle," Craig continued. "Their voices carried through easily. They were talking about some missing papers. And John was mentioned a couple of times."

"What kind of papers?"

"That wasn't very clear. But these papers were important to them. One of the guys sounded angry. Their conversation heated up. I was afraid they might come to blows."

"What happened then?" Anna asked impatiently.

"I went around and asked if they needed any help. They seemed shocked to see me. I think they had forgotten they were in a public place."

Anna wasn't interested in Craig's theories. He sensed her irritation.

"They clammed up!" He gave a big shrug. "Paid me in cash and left without a word."

"Are you sure they mentioned my John?" Anna asked urgently. "Could they have been talking about one of their friends? John's quite a common name."

"They talked about 'old John' once or twice and 'professor'. And I clearly heard them say 'Professor Butler'."

"Why didn't you tell the police about this?" Anna wanted to know.

"I had my own troubles. My son died around that time. I didn't connect the dots until those rumors about you surfaced. Even then, I thought it was too farfetched."

"You still think so, don't you?" Anna felt foolish.

Had Craig Rose concocted the whole story just so he could have something to tell her?

"It doesn't matter what I think, Mrs. Butler. Look, I have given this a lot of thought. I am sure those kids came into my store a week before your husband died. What can I say? Maybe this will open up a new line of investigation for you."

"I think it's worth pursuing." Anna felt her eyes prick with tears. "I'm grateful."

"I am the one in your debt," Craig Rose said emotionally. "My boy Finn is free of any blame, all thanks to you."

"There's a lot to be grateful for this Christmas," Anna smiled through her tears.

Craig Rose had donated a truckload of gifts for the underprivileged kids.

"We are going to the children's home later this afternoon. I'm sure your generous gifts will bring smiles to a lot of tiny faces."

"It's the least I can do." Craig Rose had a faraway look in his eyes. "My boy will never come home to open his presents."

Anna didn't know how to console him.

"You know where to find me, Craig. You will always be welcome at Anna's Café."

Craig stood up and said goodbye. Anna was surprised when

he turned around at the door and hugged her impulsively.

Anna locked the store and headed to her favorite bench on the Coastal Walk. She wasn't ready to go home yet.

The fog hanging over the bay matched her thoughts. Anna tried to process the information Craig had given her. She surmised the young men in the wine shop had been John's students. What had they wanted from him? Why were the papers they mentioned important?

Anna shivered as a sudden gust of wind swept over her. How desperate had those young men really been, she wondered.

***

Thank you for reading this book. If you enjoyed this book, please consider leaving a brief review. Even a few words or a line or two will do.

As an indie author, I rely on reviews to spread the word about my book. Your assistance will be very helpful and greatly appreciated.

I would also really appreciate it if you tell your friends and family about the book. Word of mouth is an author's best friend, and it will be of immense help to me.

Many Thanks!

Author Leena Clover

http://leenaclover.com

Leena Clover

leenaclover@gmail.com

http://twitter.com/leenaclover

https://www.facebook.com/leenaclovercozymysterybooks